I0636731

The Regimental Myna

Ruskin Bond has been writing for over sixty years, and now has over 120 titles in print—novels, collections of short stories, poetry, essays, anthologies and books for children. His first novel, *The Room on the Roof*, received the prestigious John Llewellyn Rhys Prize in 1957. He has also received the Padma Shri (1999), the Padma Bhushan (2014) and two awards from Sahitya Akademi—one for his short stories and another for his writings for children. In 2012, the Delhi government gave him its Lifetime Achievement Award.

Born in 1934, Ruskin Bond grew up in Jamnagar, Shimla, New Delhi and Dehradun. Apart from three years in the UK, he has spent all his life in India, and now lives in Mussoorie with his adopted family.

The Regimental Myna

Selected and Compiled by

RUSKIN BOND

RUPA

Published by
Rupa Publications India Pvt. Ltd 2017
7/16, Ansari Road, Daryaganj
New Delhi 110002

Sales centres:
Allahabad Bengaluru Chennai
Hyderabad Jaipur Kathmandu
Kolkata Mumbai

ISBN: 978-81-291-4749-3

First impression 2017

10 9 8 7 6 5 4 3 2 1

Printed and bound in India by Repro Knowledgecast Limited, Thane

CONTENTS

INTRODUCTION

As I sit down to write this, in front of me lies an omnibus edition of another book of humour. *A Century of Humour*, edited by P.G. Wodehouse, is a fat book and contains some excellent humorous pieces, some dating back to the early days of the twentieth century. Wodehouse was one of the world's foremost humour writers, and his novels, stories and essays have delighted generations of readers. Even now, when I wonder if anyone finds him funny or relevant, I come across a fellow fan who knows lines from his books by heart and can have an entire conversation about Blandings Castle and the Earl of Emsworth. I do believe that there are a few Wodehouse societies flourishing in some Indian cities where people meet and discuss this forever delightful writer.

In this collection, however, I have not been able to include a piece by Wodehouse. But there are plenty others to entertain the readers. There is Saki, who always had a place among the great short story and humour writers. 'The Guest' is a drily funny account of the Bishop as a particularly annoying guest with a surprise visitation of a goat-eating leopard in the end. Mark Twain was another person known for his wit and his pithy observations about human nature are sharply true. Here, I have 'What Stumped the Bluejays'. Just this description of the correct use of grammar by bluejays is enough to make one smile:

> You may say a cat uses good grammar. Well, a cat does—
> but you let a cat get excited once; you let a cat get to
> pulling fur with another cat on a shed, nights, and you'll
> hear grammar that will give you the lockjaw. Ignorant
> people think it's the noise which fighting cats make that is
> so aggravating, but it ain't so; it's the sickening grammar
> they use. Now I've never heard a jay use bad grammar
> but very seldom; and when they do, they are as ashamed
> as a human; they shut right down and leave.

Black humour is another fascinating aspect of humour writing.
To take something that is completely macabre, like in Amborse
Bierce's story 'My Favourite Murder' and make it uncomfortably
funny takes quite some talent. Also included here is one of
favourite writers, Charles Dickens and his 'The Haunted House'
which was part of his Christmas stories collection.

One does not instinctively think of the Russian writers
as humorists, but Anton Chekhov was quite the master of it.
I have always thoroughly enjoyed his story 'The Death of a
Government Clerk', about the sad yet funny fate of a man
who happens to sneeze at the wrong time and wrong place.
Similarly, there is a story by Nikolai Gogol here, and together,
I hope they make more readers turn to the Russians not just
for grim tragedies but for a bit of sharp satire too.

'The Regimental Myna' is a story I wrote many years ago
about a myna who makes an army regiment its home. Along
with a story about the always entertaining Uncle Ken, I hope
all the pieces included in this collection will make the reader
think, laugh and finally close the book with a smile on their face.

Ruskin Bond

The Regimental Myna

Ruskin Bond

In my grandfather's time, British soldiers stationed in India were very fond of keeping pets, and there were few barrack-rooms where pets were not to be found. Dogs and cats were the most common, but birds were also great favourites.

In one instance, a bird was not only the pet of a barrack-room but of a whole regiment. His owner was my grandfather, Private Bond, a soldier of the line who had come out to India with the King's Own Scottish Rifles.

The bird was a myna, common enough in India, and Grandfather named it Dickens after his favourite author. Dickens came into Grandfather's possession when quite young, and he was soon a favourite with all the men in the barracks at Meerut, where the regiment was stationed. Meerut was hot and dusty; the curries were hot and spicy; the General in command was hot-tempered and crusty. Keeping a pet was almost the sole recreation for the men in barracks.

Because he was tamed so young, Dickens (or Dicky for short) never learned to pick up food for himself. Instead, just like a baby bird, he took his meals from Grandfather's mouth. And other men used to feed him in the same way. When Dickens was hungry, he asked for food by sitting on Grandfather's shoulders, flapping his wings rapidly, and opening his beak.

Dicky was never caged, and as soon as he was able to fly he attended all parades, watched the rations being issued, and was present on every occasion which brought the soldiers out of their barracks. When out in the country, he would follow the regiment or party, flying from shoulder to shoulder, or from tree to tree, always keeping a sharp look-out for his enemies, the hawks.

Sometimes he would choose a mounted officer as a companion; but after the manoeuvres were over he would return to Grandfather's shoulder.

One day there was to be a General's inspection, and the Colonel gave orders that Dicky was to be confined, so that he wouldn't appear on parade.

'Lock him away somewhere, Bond,' the Colonel snapped. We can't have him flapping all over the parade-ground.'

Dickens was put into a storeroom, with the windows closed and the door locked. But while the General's inspection was going on, the mess orderly, who wanted something from the storeroom and knew where to find the key, opened the door.

Out flew Dickens. He made straight for the parade-ground, greatly excited at being let out and chattering loudly.

Dicky must have thought the General had something to do with his detention, or else he may have felt an explanation was due to him. Whatever his reasoning, he chose to alight on the General's pith helmet, between the plumes.

Here he chattered faster than ever, much to the surprise of the General, who was obliged to take his helmet off before he could dislodge the bird.

'What the Dickens!' exclaimed the General, going purple

in the face—for Dicky had discharged his breakfast between the plumes of the helmet.

Meanwhile, Dicky had flown to the Colonel's shoulder to make further complaints, to the great delight of the men.

'Fall out, Bond!' the Colonel screamed. 'Take this bird away—for good! I don't want to see it again!'

A crestfallen Private Bond returned to the barracks with Dicky, wondering what to do next. To part with Dicky, or even to cage him, was out of the question.

But Grandfather was not the only one who loved Dickens. He was also extremely popular with the entire battalion. In the end, Grandfather decided to ask his Captain to bring him before the Colonel so he could ask forgiveness for Dicky's behaviour.

The Colonel gave Private Bond and his Captain a patient hearing. Then the Colonel consulted his officers and decided that the bird could stay—provided he was taken on as a serving member of the regiment!

Dickens' popularity was not surprising, as he was highly intelligent. He knew the men of his own regiment from those of others, and would only associate with the Scottish Rifles. Even in the drill season, when there were as many as twenty regiments in camp, Dicky never made a mistake.

Dickens had a unique method of getting from one part of the camp to another. Instead of flying over the top of the camp, he would go in stages from tent to tent, flying very low, sheltering in each one, then peeping out and looking carefully for hawks before moving on to the next.

One day, Grandfather was admitted to hospital with malaria. Dicky couldn't find him anywhere, and searched and searched all over the camp in great distress. The hospital was a couple of kilometres away from the barracks, and it wasn't until the third day of searching that Dickens finally discovered Grandfather lying there.

From then on, for as long as Grandfather was on the sick list, Dicky spent his time at the hospital. An upturned helmet was placed on a shelf for him near Grandfather's bed, and Dickens spent the night inside it. As soon as Grandfather was discharged from the hospital, Dickens left as well, and never returned, not even for a visit.

In 1888, the regiment got orders to proceed to Calcutta, en route for Burma, where it was to take part in the Chin Lushai Expedition. All pets had to be, left behind, and Dickens was no exception.

But Dicky had his own views on the subject.

The regiment travelled in stages, marching along the Grand Trunk Road, moving at night and going into rest camps for the day.

Dickens caught up on the third day. He arrived in camp after a journey of more than three hundred kilometres—dull, dejected and starving, as he still depended on being fed from Grandfather's mouth.

Route-marching and travelling by train (the railway was just beginning to spread across India), the battalion finally reached Calcutta. From there, contrary to orders, Dickens embarked for Burma along with the soldiers.

On board the ship, Dickens would amuse himself by peeping from the portholes, and flapping from one to the other. He would also go up on deck, and sometimes even took experimental flights out to sea. But one day he was caught in a gale and had such difficulty getting back to the ship that he gave up that kind of adventuring.

Dickens stayed with his regiment all through the expedition

and the campaign. Many of his soldier friends lost their lives, but Grandfather and Dickens survived the fighting and returned safely to Calcutta.

Grandfather, now a Corporal, was given six months' home leave, along with the rest of the regiment. This meant sailing home to England.

During the first part of the voyage, Dicky was his usual cheerful self. But when the ship left the Suez Canal, the weather grew cold, and he was no longer to be seen on the yardarms or on the bridge with the captain. He even lost interest in going on deck with Grandfather, preferring to stay with the parrots on the waste deck.

After the ship passed Gibraltar, Dickens went below. He never came on deck again.

Dickens was laid out in a Huntley and Palmer's biscuit tin, and buried at sea. Not, perhaps, with full military honours, but certainly to the sound of Grandfather's bagpipes, playing *The Last Post*.

THE GUESTS

Saki

'The landscape seen from our windows is certainly charming,' said Annabel, 'those cherry orchards and green meadows, and the river winding along the valley, and the church tower peeping out among the elms, they all make a most effective picture. There's something dreadfully sleepy and languorous about it, though; stagnation seems to be the dominant note. Nothing ever happens here; seedtime and harvest, an occasional outbreak of measles or a mildly destructive thunderstorm, and a little election excitement about once in five years, that is all that we have to modify the monotony of our existence. Rather dreadful, isn't it?'

'On the contrary,' said Matilda, 'I find it soothing and restful; but then, you see, I've lived in countries where things do happen, ever so many at a time, when you're not ready for them happening all at once.'

'That, of course, makes a difference,' said Annabel.

'I have never forgotten,' said Matilda, 'the occasion when the Bishop of Bequar paid us an unexpected visit; he was on his way to lay the foundation stone of a mission-house or something of the sort.'   .

'I thought that out there you were always prepared for emergency guests turning up,' said Annabel.

'I was quite prepared for half a dozen Bishops,' said Matilda, 'but it was rather disconcerting to find out after a little conversation that this particular one was a distant cousin of mine, belonging to a branch of the family that had quarrelled bitterly and offensively with our branch about a Crown Derby dessert service; they got it, and we ought to have got it, in some legacy, or else we got it and they thought they ought to have it, I forget which; anyhow, I know they behaved disgracefully. Now here was one of them turning up in the odour of sanctity, so to speak, and claiming the traditional hospitality of the East.'

'It was rather trying, but you could have left your husband to do most of the entertaining.'

'My husband was fifty miles up-country, talking sense, or what he imagined to be sense, to a village community that fancied one of their leading men was a were-tiger.'

'A what tiger?'

'A were-tiger; you've heard of were-wolves, haven't you, a mixture of wolf and human being and demon? Well, in those parts they have were-tigers, or think they have, and I must say that in this case, so far as sworn and uncontested evidence went, they had every ground for thinking so. However, as we gave up witchcraft prosecutions about three hundred years ago, we don't like to have other people keeping on our discarded practices; it doesn't seem respectful to our mental and moral position.'

'I hope you weren't unkind to the Bishop,' said Annabel.

'Well, of course he was my guest, so I had to be outwardly polite to him, but he was tactless enough to rake up the incidents of the old quarrel, and to try to make out that there was something to be said for the way his side of the family had behaved; even if there was, which I don't for a moment admit, my house was not the place in which to say it. I didn't argue the matter, but I gave my cook a holiday to go and visit his aged parents some ninety miles away. The emergency cook was not a specialist in curries, in fact, I don't think cooking in any shape or form could have been one of his strong points. I believe he originally came to us in the guise of a gardener, but as we never pretended to have anything that could be considered a garden he was utilized as assistant goatherd, in which capacity, I understand, he gave every satisfaction. When the Bishop heard that I had sent away the cook on a special and unnecessary holiday he saw the inwardness of the manoeuvre, and from that moment we were scarcely on speaking terms. If you have ever had a Bishop with whom you were not on speaking terms staying in your house, you will appreciate the situation.'

Annabel confessed that her life story had never included such a disturbing experience.

'Then,' continued Matilda, 'to make matters more complicated, the Gwadlipichee overflowed its banks, a thing it did every now and then when the rains were unduly prolonged, and the lower part of the house and all the out-buildings were submerged. We managed to get the ponies loose in time, and the syce swam the whole lot of them off to the nearest rising ground. A goat or two, the chief goatherd, the chief goatherd's wife, and several of their babies came to anchorage in the verandah. All the rest of the available space was filled up with wet, bedraggled-looking hens and chickens; one never really knows how many fowls one possesses till the servants' quarters are flooded out. Of course, I had been through something of the sort in previous floods, but never before had I had a houseful of goats and babies and half-drowned hens, supplemented by a

Bishop with whom I was hardly on speaking terms.'

'It must have been a trying experience,' commented Annabel.

'More embarrassments were to follow. I wasn't going to let a mere ordinary flood wash out the memory of that Crown Derby dessert service, and I intimated to the Bishop that his large bedroom, with a writing table in it, and his small bathroom, with a sufficiency of cold water jars in it, was his share of the premises, and that space was rather congested under the existing circumstances. However, at about three o'clock in the afternoon, when he had awakened from his midday sleep, he made a sudden incursion into the room that was normally the drawing-room, but was now dining-room, store-house, saddle-room, and half a dozen other temporary premises as well. From the condition of my guest's costume he seemed to think it might also serve as his dressing-room.

"I'm afraid there is nowhere for you to sit,' I said coldly; 'the verandah is full of goats.'

"There is a goat in my bedroom,' he observed with equal coldness, and more than a suspicion of sardonic reproach.

"Really,' I said, 'another survivor? I thought all the other goats were done for.'

"This particular goat is quite done for,' he said, 'it is being devoured by a leopard at the present moment. That is why I left the room; some animals resent being watched while they are eating.'

'The leopard, of course, was easily explained; it had been hanging round the goat sheds when the flood came, and had clambered up by the outside staircase leading to the Bishop's bathroom, thoughtfully bringing a goat with it. Probably it found the bathroom too damp and shut-in for its taste, and transferred its banqueting operations to the bedroom while the Bishop was having his nap.'

'What a frightful situation!' exclaimed Annabel; 'fancy having a ravening leopard in the house, with a flood all round you.'

'Not in the least ravening,' said Matilda; 'it was full of goat, had any amount of water at its disposal if it felt thirsty, and probably had no more immediate wish than a desire for uninterrupted sleep. Still, I think anyone will admit that it was an embarrassing predicament to have your only available guest-room occupied by a leopard, the verandah choked up with goats and babies and wet hens, and a Bishop with whom you were scarcely on speaking terms planted down in your own sitting-room. I really don't know how I got through those crawling hours, and of course mealtimes only made matters worse. The emergency cook had every excuse for sending in watery soup and sloppy rice, and as neither the chief goat-herd nor his wife were expert divers, the cellar could not be reached. Fortunately, the Gwadlipichee subsides as rapidly as it rises, and just before dawn the syce came splashing back, with the ponies only fetlock deep in water. Then there arose some awkwardness from the fact that the Bishop wished to leave sooner than the leopard did, and as the latter was ensconced in the midst of the former's personal possessions there was an obvious difficulty in altering the order of departure. I pointed out to the Bishop that a leopard's habits and tastes are not those of an otter, and that it naturally preferred walking to wading; and that in any case a meal of an entire goat, washed down with tub water, justified a certain amount of repose; if I had had guns fired to frighten the animal away, as the Bishop suggested, it would probably merely have left the bedroom to come into the already overcrowded drawing-room. Altogether it was rather a relief when they both left. Now, perhaps, you can understand my appreciation of a sleepy countryside where things don't happen.'

WHAT STUMPED THE BLUEJAYS

Mark Twain

Animals talk to each other, of course. There can be no question about that; but I suppose there are very few people who can understand them. I never knew but one man who could. I knew he could, however, because he told me so himself. He was a middle-aged, simple-hearted miner who had lived in a lonely corner of California, among the woods and mountains, a good many years, and had studied the ways of his only neighbours, the beasts and the birds, until he believed he could accurately translate any remark which they made. This was Jim Baker. According to Jim Baker, some animals have only a limited education, and use only very simple words, and scarcely ever a comparison or a flowery figure; whereas, certain other animals have a large vocabulary, a fine command of language and a ready and fluent delivery; consequently these latter talk a great deal; they like it; they are conscious of their talent, and they enjoy 'showing off'. Baker said, that after long and careful observation, he had come to the conclusion that the bluejays were the best talkers he had found among birds and beasts. He said:

'There's more to a bluejay than any other creature. He has

got more moods, and more different kinds of feelings than other creatures; and mind you, whatever a bluejay feels, he can put into language. And no mere commonplace language, either, but rattling, out-and-out book talk—and bristling with metaphor, too—just bristling! And as for command of language—why you never see a bluejay get stuck for a word. No man ever did. They just boil out of him! And another thing: I've noticed a good deal, and there's no bird, or cow, or anything that uses as good grammar as a bluejay. You may say a cat uses good grammar. Well, a cat does—but you let a cat get excited once; you let a cat get to pulling fur with another cat on a shed, nights, and you'll hear grammar that will give you the lockjaw. Ignorant people think it's the noise which fighting cats make that is so aggravating, but it ain't so; it's the sickening grammar they use. Now I've never heard a jay use bad grammar but very seldom; and when they do, they are as ashamed as a human; they shut right down and leave.

'You may call a jay a bird. Well, so he is, in a measure—because he's got feathers on him, and don't belong to no church, perhaps; but otherwise he is just as much a human as you be. And I'll tell you for why. A jay's gifts, instincts, feelings and interests cover the whole ground. A jay hasn't got any more principle than a congressman. A jay will lie, a jay will steal, a jay will deceive, a jay will betray; and four times out of five, a jay will go back on his solemnest promise. The sacredness of an obligation is a thing which you can't cram into no bluejay's head. Now, on top of all this, there's another thing; a jay can outswear any gentleman in the mines. You think a cat can swear. Well, a cat can; but you give a bluejay a subject that calls for his reserve powers, and where is your cat! Don't talk to me—I know too much about this thing. And there's yet another thing;

in the one little particular of scolding—just good, clean, out-and-out scolding—a bluejay can lay over anything, human or divine. Yes, sir, a jay is everything that a man is. A jay can cry, a jay can laugh, a jay can feel shame, a jay can reason and plan and discuss, a jay likes gossip and scandal, a jay has got a sense of humor, a jay knows when he is an ass just as well as you do—maybe better. If a jay ain't human, he better take in his sign, that's all. Now I'm going to tell you a perfectly true fact about some bluejays. When I first begun to understand jay language correctly, there was a little incident happened here. Seven years ago, the last man in this region but he moved away. There stands his house—been empty ever since; a log house, with a plank roof—just one big room, and no more; no ceiling—nothing between the rafters and the floor. Well, one Sunday morning I was sitting out here in front of my cabin, with my cat, taking the sun, and looking at the blue hills, and listening to the leaves rustling so lonely in the trees, and thinking of the home away yonder in the States, that I hadn't heard from in thirteen years, when a bluejay lit on that house, with an acorn in his mouth, and says, "Hello, I reckon I've struck something." When he spoke, the acorn dropped out of his mouth and rolled down the roof, of course, but he didn't care; his mind was all on the thing he had struck. It was a knothole in the roof. He cocked his head to one side, shut one eye and put the other one to the hole, like a possum looking down a jug; then he glanced up with his bright eyes, gave a wink or two with his wings—which signifies gratification, you understand—and says, "It looks like a hole, it's located like a hole—blamed if I don't believe it is a hole!"

'Then he cocked his head down and took another look; he glances up perfectly joyful, this time; winks his wings and his tail both, and says, "Oh, no, this ain't no fat thing, I reckon! If I ain't in luck! Why it's a perfectly elegant hole!" So he flew down and got that acorn, and fetched it up and dropped it in, and was just tilting his head back, with the heavenliest smile on his face, when all of a sudden he was paralyzed into a listening attitude and that smile faded gradually out of his countenance like breath off'n a razor, and the queerest look of surprise took its place. Then he says, "Why, I didn't hear it fall!" He cocked his eye at the hole again, and took a long look; raised up and shook his head; stepped around to the other side of the hole and took another look from that side; shook his head again. He studied awhile, then he just went into the details—walked round and round the hole and spied into it from every point of the compass. No use. Now he took a thinking attitude on the comb of the roof and scratched the back of his head with his right foot a minute, and finally says, "Well, it's too many for me, that's certain; must be a mighty long hole; however, I ain't got no time to fool around here, I got to tend to business; I reckon it's all right—chance it, anyway."

'So he flew off and fetched another acorn and dropped it in, and tried to flirt his eye to the hole quick enough to see what become of it, but he was too late. He held his eye there as much as a minute; then he raised up and sighed, and says, "Confound it, I don't seem to understand this thing, no way; however, I'll tackle her again." He fetched another acorn, and done his level best to see what become of it, but he couldn't. He says, "Well, I never struck no such a hole as this before; I'm of the opinion it's a totally new kind of a hole." Then he begun to get mad. He held in for a spell, walking up and down the comb of the roof and shaking his head and muttering to himself; but his feelings got the upper hand of him, presently, and he broke loose and cussed himself black in the face. I never see a bird take on so about a little thing. When he got through he walks to the hole and looks in again for half a minute; then he says, "Well, you're a long hole, and a deep hole, and a mighty singular hole altogether—but I've started in to fill you, and I'm determined if I don't fill you, if it takes a hundred years!"

'And with that, away he went. You never see a bird work so since you were born. The way he hove acorns into that hole for about two hours and a half was one of the most exciting and astonishing spectacles I ever struck. He never stopped to take a look anymore—he just hove'em in and went for more. Well, at last he could hardly flop his wings, he was so tuckered out. He comes a-drooping down, once more, sweating like an ice pitcher, drops his acorn in and says, "Now I guess I've got the bulge on you by this time!" So he bent down for a look. If you'll believe me, when his head came up again he was just pale with rage. He says, "I've shoveled acorns enough in there to keep the family thirty years, and if I can see a sign of one of'em I wish I may land in a museum with a belly full of sawdust in two minutes!"

'He just had strength enough to crawl up onto the comb and lean his back again the chimbly, and then he collected his impressions and begun to free his mind. I see in a second that what I had mistook for profanity in the mines was only just the rudiments, as you may say.

'Another jay was going by, and heard him doing his devotions, and stops to inquire what was up. The sufferer told him the whole circumstance, and says, "Now yonder's the hole, and if you don't believe me, go and look for yourself." So this fellow went and looked, and comes back and says, "How many did you say you put in there?" "Not any less than two tons," says the sufferer. The other jay went and looked again. He couldn't seem to make it out, so he raised a yell, and three more jays come. They all examined the hole, they all made the sufferer tell it over again, then they all discussed it, and got off as many leather-headed opinions about it as an average crowd of humans could have done.

'They called in more jays; then more and more, till pretty soon this whole region beared to have a blue flush about it. There must have been five thousand of them; and such another jawing and disputing and ripping and cussing, you never heard. Every jay in the whole lot put his eye to the hole and delivered a more chuckle-headed opinion about the mystery than the jay that went there before him. They examined the house all over, too. The door was standing half open, and at last one old jay happened to go and light on it and look in. Of course, that knocked the mystery galley-west in a second. There lay the acorns, scattered all over the floor. He flopped his wings and raised a whoop. "Come here!" he says. "Come here, everybody; hang'd if this fool hasn't been trying to fill up a house with acorns!" They all came a-swooping down like a blue cloud, and as each fellow lit on the door and took a glance, the whole absurdity of the contract that that first jay had tackled hit him home and he fell over backward suffocating with laughter, and the next jay took his place and did the same.

'Well, sir, they roosted around here on the housetop and the trees for an hour, and guffawed over that thing like human beings. It ain't any use to tell me a bluejay hasn't got a sense of humour, because I know better. And memory, too. They brought jays here from all over the United States to look down that hole, every summer for three years. Other birds, too. And they could all see the point, except an owl that come from

Nova Scotia to visit the Yosemite, and he took this thing in on his way back. He said he couldn't see anything funny in it. But then he was a good deal disappointed about Yosemite, too.

THE MODEL MILLIONAIRE:
Note of Admiration

Oscar Wilde

Unless one is wealthy there is no use in being a charming fellow. Romance is the privilege of the rich, not the profession of the unemployed. The poor should be practical and prosaic. It is better to have a permanent income than to be fascinating. These are the great truths of modern life which Hughie Erskine never realized. Poor Hughie! Intellectually, we must admit, he was not of much importance. He never said a brilliant or even an ill-natured thing in his life. But then he was wonderfully good-looking, with his crisp brown hair, his clear-cut profile, and his grey eyes. He was as popular with men as he was with women, and he had every accomplishment except that of making money. His father had bequeathed him his cavalry sword, and a *History of the Peninsular War* in fifteen volumes. Hughie hung the first over his looking-glass, put the second on a shelf between *Ruff's Guide* and *Bailey's Magazine*, and lived on two hundred a year that an old aunt allowed him. He had tried everything. He had gone on the Stock Exchange for six months; but what was a butterfly to do among bulls and bears? He had been a tea-merchant for a little longer, but had soon tired of pekoe and souchong. Then he had tried selling dry sherry. That did not answer; the sherry was a little too dry. Ultimately he became nothing, a delightful, ineffectual young man with a perfect profile and no profession.

To make matters worse, he was in love. The girl he loved was Laura Merton, the daughter of a retired Colonel who had lost his temper and his digestion in India, and had never found either of them again. Laura adored him, and he was ready to kiss her shoe-strings. They were the handsomest couple in London, and had not a penny-piece between them. The Colonel was very fond of Hughie, but would not hear of any engagement.

'Come to me, my boy, when you have got ten thousand pounds of your own, and we will see about it,' he used to say; and Hughie looked very glum on those days, and had to go to Laura for consolation.

One morning, as he was on his way to Holland Park, where the Mertons lived, he dropped in to see a great friend of his, Alan Trevor. Trevor was a painter. Indeed, few people escape that nowadays. But he was also an artist, and artists are rather rare. Personally he was a strange rough fellow, with a freckled face and a red, ragged beard. However, when he took up the brush he was a real master, and his pictures were eagerly sought after. He had been very much attracted by Hughie at first, it must be acknowledged, entirely on account of his personal charm. 'The only people a painter should know,' he used to say, 'are people who are bête and beautiful, people who are an artistic pleasure to look at and an intellectual repose to talk to. Men who are dandies and women who are darlings rule the world, at least they should do so.' However, after he got to know Hughie better, he liked him quite as much for his bright buoyant spirits and his generous reckless nature, and had given him the permanent entrée to his studio.

When Hughie came in he found Trevor putting the finishing touches to a wonderful life-size picture of a beggar-man. The beggar himself was standing on a raised platform in a corner of the studio. He was a wizened old man, with a face like wrinkled parchment, and a most piteous expression. Over his shoulders was flung a coarse brown cloak, all tears and tatters; his thick boots were patched and cobbled, and with one hand he leaned on a rough stick, while with the other he held out his battered hat for alms.

'What an amazing model!' whispered Hughie, as he shook hands with his friend.

'An amazing model?' shouted Trevor at the top of his voice; 'I should think so! Such beggars as he are not to be met with every day. A *trouvaille, mort cher*; a living Velasquez! My stars! what an etching Rembrandt would have made of him!'

'Poor old chap! said Hughie, 'how miserable he looks! But I suppose, to you painters, his face is his fortune?'

'Certainly,' replied Trevor, 'you don't want a beggar to look happy, do you?'

'How much does a model get for sitting?' asked Hughie, as he found himself a comfortable seat on a divan.

'A shilling an hour.'

'And how much do you get for your picture, Alan?'

'Oh, for this I get two thousand!'

'Pounds?'

'Guineas. Painters, poets, and physicians always get guineas.'

'Well, I think the model should have a percentage,' cried Hughie, laughing; 'they work quite as hard as you do.'

'Nonsense, nonsense! Why, look at the trouble of laying on the paint alone, and standing all day long at one's easel!

It's all very well, Hughie, for you to talk, but I assure you that there are moments when art almost attains to the dignity of manual labour. But you mustn't chatter; I'm very busy. Smoke a cigarette, and keep quiet.'

After some time the servant came in, and told Trevor that the frame-maker wanted to speak to him.

'Don't run away, Hughie,' he said, as he went out, 'I will be back in a moment.'

The old beggar-man took advantage of Trevor's absence to rest for a moment on a wooden bench that was behind him. He looked so forlorn and wretched that Hughie could not help pitying him, and felt in his pockets to see what money he had. All he could find was a sovereign and some coppers. 'Poor old fellow,' he thought to himself, 'he wants it more than I do, but it means no hansoms for a fortnight;' and he walked across the studio and slipped the sovereign into the beggar's hand.

The old man stared, and a faint smile flitted across his withered lips. 'Thank you, sir,' he said, 'thank you.'

Then Trevor arrived, and Hughie took his leave, blushing a little at what he had done. He spent the day with Laura, got a charming scolding for his extravagance, and had to walk home.

That night he strolled into the Palette Club about eleven o'clock, and found Trevor sitting by himself in the smoking-room drinking hock and seltzer.

'Well, Alan, did you get the picture finished all right?' he said, as he lit his cigarette.

'Finished and framed, my boy!' answered Trevor; 'and, by-the-bye, you have made a conquest. That old model you saw is quite devoted to you. I had to tell him all about you—who you are, where you live, what your income is, what prospects you have—'

'My dear Alan,' cried Hughie, 'I shall probably find him waiting for me when I go home. But of course you are only joking. Poor old wretch! I wish I could do something for him. I think it is dreadful that any one should be so miserable. I have got heaps of old clothes at home—do you think he would care for any of them? Why, his rags were falling to bits.'

'But he looks splendid in them,' said Trevor. 'I wouldn't paint him in a frock-coat for anything. What you call rags I call romance. What seems poverty to you is picturesqueness to me. However, I'll tell him of your offer.'

'Alan,' said Hughie seriously, 'you painters are a heartless lot.'

'An artist's heart is his head,' replied Trevor; 'and besides, our business is to realize the world as we see it, not to reform it as we know it. *À chacun son métier*. And now tell me how Laura is. The old model was quite interested in her.'

'You don't mean to say you talked to him about her?' said Hughie.

'Certainly I did. He knows all about the relentless colonel, the lovely Laura, and the £10,000.'

'You told that old beggar all my private affairs?' cried Hughie, looking very red and angry.

'My dear boy,' said Trevor, smiling, 'that old beggar, as you call him, is one of the richest men in Europe. He could buy all London tomorrow without overdrawing his account. He has a house in every capital, dines off gold plate, and can prevent Russia going to war when he chooses.'

'What on earth do you mean?' exclaimed Hughie.

'What I say,' said Trevor. 'The old man you saw today in the studio was Baron Hausberg. He is a great friend of mine, buys all my pictures and that sort of thing, and gave me a commission a month ago to paint him as a beggar. *Que voulez-*

vous? La fantaisie d'un millionnaire! And I must say he made a magnificent figure in his rags, or perhaps I should say in my rags; they are an old suit I got in Spain.'

'Baron Hausberg!' cried Hughie. 'Good heavens! I gave him a sovereign!' and he sank into an armchair the picture of dismay.

'Gave him a sovereign!' shouted Trevor, and he burst into a roar of laughter. 'My dear boy, you'll never see it again. *Son affaire c'est l'argent des autres.*'

'I think you might have told me, Alan,' said Hughie sulkily, 'and not have let me make such a fool of myself.'

'Well, to begin with, Hughie,' said Trevor, 'it never entered my mind that you went about distributing alms in that reckless way. I can understand your kissing a pretty model, but your giving a sovereign to an ugly one—by Jove, no! Besides, the fact is that I really was not at home today to anyone; and when you came in I didn't know whether Hausberg would like his name mentioned. You know he wasn't in full dress.'

'What a duffer he must think me!' said Hughie.

'Not at all. He was in the highest spirits after you left; kept chuckling to himself and rubbing his old wrinkled hands together. I couldn't make out why he was so interested to know all about you; but I see it all now. He'll invest your sovereign for you, Hughie, pay you the interest every six months, and have a capital story to tell after dinner.'

'I am an unlucky devil,' growled Hughie. 'The best thing I can do is to go to bed; and, my dear Alan, you mustn't tell anyone. I shouldn't dare show my face in the Row.'

'Nonsense! It reflects the highest credit on your philanthropic spirit, Hughie. And don't run away. Have another cigarette, and you can talk about Laura as much as you like.'

However, Hughie wouldn't stop, but walked home, feeling

very unhappy, and leaving Alan Trevor in fits of laughter.

The next morning, as he was at breakfast, the servant brought him up a card on which was written, 'Monsieur Gustave Naudin, *de la part de* M. le Baron Hausberg.'

'I suppose he has come for an apology,' said Hughie to himself; and he told the servant to show the visitor up.

An old gentleman with gold spectacles and grey hair came into the room, and said, in a slight French accent, 'Have I the honour of addressing Monsieur Erskine?'

Hughie bowed.

'I have come from Baron Hausberg,' he continued. 'The Baron—'

'I beg, sir, that you will offer him my sincerest apologies,' stammered Hughie.

'The Baron,' said the old gentleman, with a smile, 'has commissioned me to bring you this letter;' and he extended a sealed envelope.

On the outside was written, 'A wedding present to Hugh Erskine and Laura Merton, from an old beggar,' and inside was a cheque for £10,000.

When they were married, Alan Trevor was the best man, and the Baron made a speech at the wedding breakfast.

'Millionaire models,' remarked Alan, 'are rare enough; but, by Jove, model millionaires are rarer still!'

MY FAVOURITE MURDER

Ambrose Bierce

Having murdered my mother under circumstances of singular atrocity, I was arrested and put upon my trial, which lasted seven years. In charging the jury, the judge of the Court of Acquittal remarked that it was one of the most ghastly crimes that he had ever been called upon to explain away.

At this, my attorney rose and said:

'May it please your Honour, crimes are ghastly or agreeable only by comparison. If you were familiar with the details of my client's previous murder of his uncle you would discern in his later offence (if offence it may be called) something in the nature of tender forbearance and filial consideration for the feelings of the victim. The appalling ferocity of the former assassination was indeed inconsistent with any hypothesis but that of guilt; and had it not been for the fact that the honourable judge before whom he was tried was the president of a life insurance company that took risks on hanging, and in which my client held a policy, it is hard to see how he could decently have been acquitted. If your honour would like to hear about it for instruction and guidance of your Honour's mind, this unfortunate man, my client, will consent to give himself the pain of relating it under oath.'

The district attorney said: 'Your Honour, I object. Such a statement would be in the nature of evidence, and the testimony in this case is closed. The prisoner's statement should have been introduced three years ago, in the spring of 1881.'

'In a statutory sense,' said the judge, 'you are right, and in the Court of Objections and Technicalities you would get a ruling in your favour. But not in a Court of Acquittal. The objection is overruled.'

'I except,' said the district attorney.

'You cannot do that,' the judge said. 'I must remind you that in order to take an exception you must first get this case transferred for a time to the Court of Exceptions on a formal motion duly supported by affidavits. A motion to that effect by your predecessor in office was denied by me during the first year of this trial. Mr Clerk, swear the prisoner.'

The customary oath having been administered, I made the following statement, which impressed the judge with so strong a sense of the comparative triviality of the offence for which I was on trial that he made no further search for mitigating circumstances, but simply instructed the jury to acquit, and I left the court, without a stain upon my reputation:

'I was born in 1856 in Kalamakee, Mich., of honest and reputable parents, one of whom Heaven has mercifully spared to comfort me in my later years. In 1867 the family came to California and settled near Nigger Head, where my father opened a road agency and prospered beyond the dreams of avarice. He was a reticent, saturnine man then, though his increasing years have now somewhat relaxed the austerity of his disposition, and I believe that nothing but his memory of the sad event for which I am now on trial prevents him from manifesting a genuine hilarity.

'Four years after we had set up the road agency an itinerant preacher came along, and having no other way to pay for the night's lodging that we gave him, favoured us with an exhortation of such power that, praise God, we were all converted to religion. My father at once sent for his brother the Hon. William Ridley of Stockton, and on his arrival turned over the agency to him, charging him nothing for the franchise nor plant—the latter consisting of a Winchester rifle, a sawed-off shotgun, and an assortment of masks made out of flour sacks. The family then moved to Ghost Rock and opened a dance house. It was called 'The Saints' Rest Hurdy-Gurdy,' and the proceedings each night began with prayer. It was there that my now sainted mother, by her grace in the dance, acquired the sobriquet of 'The Bucking Walrus'.

'In the fall of '75 I had occasion to visit Coyote, on the road to Mahala, and took the stage at Ghost Rock. There were four other passengers. About three miles beyond Nigger Head, persons whom I identified as my Uncle William and his two sons held up the stage. Finding nothing in the express box, they went through the passengers. I acted a most Honourable part in the affair, placing myself in line with the others, holding up my hands and permitting myself to be deprived of forty dollars and a gold watch. From my behaviour no one could have suspected that I knew the gentlemen who gave the entertainment. A few days later, when I went to Nigger Head and asked for the return of my money and watch my uncle and cousins swore they knew nothing of the matter, and they affected a belief that my father and I had done the job ourselves in dishonest violation of commercial good faith. Uncle William even threatened to retaliate by starting an opposition dance house at Ghost Rock.

As 'The Saints' Rest' had become rather unpopular, I saw that this would assuredly ruin it and prove a paying enterprise, so I told my uncle that I was willing to overlook the past if he would take me into the scheme and keep the partnership a secret from my father. This fair offer he rejected, and I then perceived that it would be better and more satisfactory if he were dead.

'My plans to that end were soon perfected, and communicating them to my dear parents I had the gratification of receiving their approval. My father said he was proud of me, and my mother promised that although her religion forbade her to assist in taking human life I should have the advantage of her prayers for my success. As a preliminary measure looking to my security in case of detection I made an application for membership in that powerful order, the Knights of Murder, and in due course was received as a member of the Ghost Rock commandery. On the day that my probation ended I was for the first time permitted to inspect the records of the order and learn who belonged to it—all the rites of initiation having been conducted in masks. Fancy my delight when, in looking over the roll of membership, I found the third name to be that of my uncle, who indeed was junior vice-chancellor of the order! Here was an opportunity exceeding my wildest dreams—to murder I could add insubordination and treachery. It was what my good mother would have called 'a special Providence'.

'At about this time something occurred which caused my cup of joy, already full, to overflow on all sides, a circular cataract of bliss. Three men, strangers in that locality, were arrested for the stage robbery in which I had lost my money and watch. They were brought to trial and, despite my efforts to clear them and fasten the guilt upon three of the most respectable and worthy citizens of Ghost Rock, convicted on the clearest proof. The murder would now be as wanton and reasonless as I could wish.

'One morning I shouldered my Winchester rifle, and going over to my uncle's house, near Nigger Head, asked my Aunt Mary, his wife, if he were at home, adding that I had come to kill him. My aunt replied with her peculiar smile that so many gentleman called on that errand and were afterward carried away without having performed it that I must excuse her for doubting my good faith in the matter. She said I did not look as if I would kill anybody, so, as a proof of good faith I levelled my rifle and wounded a Chinaman who happened to be passing the house. She said she knew whole families that could do a thing of that kind, but Bill Ridley was a horse of another colour. She said, however, that I would find him over on the other side of the creek in the sheep lot; and she added that she hoped the best man would win.

'My Aunt Mary was one of the most fair-minded women that I have ever met.

'I found my uncle down on his knees engaged in skinning a sheep. Seeing that he had neither gun nor pistol handy I had not the heart to shoot him, so I approached him, greeted him pleasantly and struck him a powerful blow on the head with the butt of my rifle. I have a very good delivery and Uncle William lay down on his side, then rolled over on his back, spread out his fingers and shivered. Before he could recover the use of his limbs I seized the knife that he had been using and cut his hamstrings. You know, doubtless, that when you sever the Achilles tendon, the patient has no further use of his leg; it is just the same as if he had no leg. Well, I parted them both, and when he revived he was at my service. As soon as he comprehended the situation, he said:

'"Samuel, you have got the drop on me and can afford to be generous. I have only one thing to ask of you, and that is that you carry me to the house and finish me in the bosom of my family."

'I told him I thought that a pretty reasonable request and I would do so if he would let me put him into a wheat sack; he would be easier to carry that way and if we were seen by the neighbours en route it would cause less remark. He agreed to that, and going to the barn I got a sack. This, however, did not fit him; it was too short and much wider than he; so I bent his legs, forced his knees up against his breast and got him into it that way, tying the sack above his head. He was a heavy man and I had all that I could do to get him on my back, but I staggered along for some distance until I came to a swing that some of the children had suspended to the branch of an oak. Here I laid him down and sat upon him to rest, and the sight of the rope gave me a happy inspiration. In twenty minutes my uncle, still in the sack, swung free to the sport of the wind.

'I had taken down the rope, tied one end tightly about the mouth of the bag, thrown the other across the limb and hauled him up about five feet from the ground. Fastening the other end of the rope also about the mouth of the sack, I had the satisfaction to see my uncle converted into a large, fine pendulum. I must add that he was not himself entirely aware of the nature of the change that he had undergone in his relation to the exterior world, though in justice to a good man's memory I ought to say that I do not think he would in any case have wasted much of my time in vain remonstrance.

'Uncle William had a ram that was famous in all that region as a fighter. It was in a state of chronic constitutional indignation. Some deep disappointment in early life had soured its disposition and it had declared war upon the whole world. To say that it would butt anything accessible is but faintly to express the nature and scope of its military activity: the universe was its antagonist; its methods that of a projectile. It fought like the angels and devils, in mid-air, cleaving the atmosphere like a bird, describing a parabolic curve and descending upon its victim at just the exact angle of incidence to make the most of its velocity and weight. Its momentum, calculated in foot-tons, was something incredible. It had been seen to destroy a four-year-old bull by a single impact upon that animal's gnarly forehead. No stone wall had ever been known to resist its downward swoop; there were no trees tough enough to stay it; it would splinter them into matchwood and defile their leafy honours in the dust. This irascible and implacable brute—this incarnate thunderbolt—this monster of the upper deep, I had seen reposing in the shade of an adjacent tree, dreaming dreams of conquest and glory. It was with a view to summoning it forth to the field of honour that I suspended its master in the manner described.

'Having completed my preparations, I imparted to the avuncular pendulum a gentle oscillation, and retiring to cover behind a contiguous rock, lifted up my voice in a long rasping cry whose diminishing final note was drowned in a noise like that of a swearing cat, which emanated from the sack. Instantly that formidable sheep was upon its feet and had taken in the military situation at a glance. In a few moments it had approached, stamping, to within fifty yards of the swinging foeman, who, now retreating and anon advancing, seemed to invite the fray. Suddenly I saw the beast's head drop earthward as if depressed by the weight of its enormous horns; then a dim, white, wavy streak of sheep prolonged itself from that spot in a generally horizontal direction to within about four yards of a point immediately beneath the enemy. There it struck sharply upward, and before it had faded from my gaze at the place whence it had set out I heard a horrid thump and a piercing scream, and my poor uncle shot forward, with a slack rope higher than the limb to which he was attached. Here the rope tautened with a jerk, arresting his flight, and back he swung in a breathless curve to the other end of his arc. The ram had fallen, a heap of indistinguishable legs, wool and horns, but pulling itself together and dodging as its antagonist swept downward it retired at random, alternately shaking its head and stamping its fore-feet. When it had backed about the same distance as that from which it had delivered the assault it paused again, bowed its head as if in prayer for victory and again shot forward, dimly visible as before—a prolonging white streak with monstrous undulations, ending with a sharp ascension. Its course this time was at a right angle to its former one, and its impatience so great that it struck the enemy before he had nearly reached the lowest point of his arc. In consequence he went flying round and round in a horizontal circle whose radius was about equal to half the length of the rope, which I forgot to say was nearly twenty feet long. His shrieks, crescendo in approach and diminuendo in recession, made the rapidity of his revolution more obvious to the ear than to the eye. He had evidently not yet been struck in a vital spot. His posture in the sack and the distance from the ground at which he hung compelled the ram to operate upon his lower extremities and the end of his back. Like a plant that has struck its root into some poisonous mineral, my poor uncle was dying slowly upward.

'After delivering its second blow the ram had not again retired. The fever of battle burned hot in its heart; its brain was intoxicated with the wine of strife. Like a pugilist who in his rage forgets his skill and fights ineffectively at half-arm's length, the angry beast endeavoured to reach its fleeting foe by awkward vertical leaps as he passed overhead, sometimes, indeed, succeeding in striking him feebly, but more frequently overthrown by its own misguided eagerness. But as the impetus was exhausted and the man's circles narrowed in scope and diminished in speed, bringing him nearer to the ground, these tactics produced better results, eliciting a superior quality of screams, which I greatly enjoyed.

'Suddenly, as if the bugles had sung truce, the ram suspended hostilities and walked away, thoughtfully wrinkling and smoothing its great aquiline nose, and occasionally cropping a bunch of grass and slowly munching it. It seemed to have tired of war's alarms and resolved to beat the sword into a plowshare and cultivate the arts of peace. Steadily, it held its course away from the field of fame until it had gained a distance of nearly a quarter of a mile. There it stopped and stood with its rear to the foe, chewing its cud and apparently half asleep. I observed, however, an occasional slight turn of its head, as if its apathy were more affected than real.

'Meantime, Uncle William's shrieks had abated with his motion, and nothing was heard from him but long, low moans, and at long intervals my name, uttered in pleading tones exceedingly grateful to my ear. Evidently the man had not the faintest notion of what was being done to him, and was inexpressibly terrified. When Death comes cloaked in mystery he is terrible indeed. Little by little my uncle's oscillations diminished, and finally he hung motionless. I went to him and was about to give him the coup de grâce, when I heard and felt a succession of smart shocks which shook the ground like a series of light earthquakes, and turning in the direction of the ram, saw a long cloud of dust approaching me with inconceivable rapidity and alarming effect! At a distance of some thirty yards away it stopped short, and from the near end of it rose into the air what I at first thought a great white bird. Its ascent was so smooth and easy and regular that I could not realize its extraordinary celerity, and was lost in admiration of its grace. To this day the impression remains that it was a slow, deliberate movement, the ram—for it was that animal—being upborne by some power other than its own impetus, and supported through the successive stages of its flight with infinite tenderness and care. My eyes followed its progress through the air with unspeakable pleasure, all the greater by contrast with my former terror of its approach by land. Onward and upward the noble animal sailed, its head bent down almost between its knees, its fore-feet thrown back, its hinder legs trailing to rear like the legs of a soaring heron.

'At a height of forty or fifty feet, as fond recollection presents it to view, it attained its zenith and appeared to remain an instant stationary; then, tilting suddenly forward without altering the relative position of its parts, it shot downward on a steeper and steeper course with augmenting velocity, passed immediately above me with a noise like the rush of a cannon shot and struck my poor uncle almost squarely on the top of the head! So frightful was the impact that not only the man's neck was broken, but the rope too; and the body of the deceased, forced against the earth, was crushed to pulp beneath the awful front of that meteoric sheep! The concussion stopped all the clocks between Lone Hand and Dutch Dan's, and Professor Davidson, a distinguished authority in matters seismic, who happened to be in the vicinity, promptly explained that the vibrations were from north to southwest.

'Altogether, I cannot help thinking that in point of artistic atrocity my murder of Uncle William has seldom been excelled.'

TITBOTTOM'S SPECTACLES

George William Curtis

Prue and I do not entertain much; our means forbid it. In truth, other people entertain for us. We enjoy that hospitality of which no account is made. We see the show, and hear the music, and smell the flowers of great festivities, tasting as it were the drippings from rich dishes. Our own dinner service is remarkably plain, our dinners, even on state occasions, are strictly in keeping, and almost our only guest is Titbottom. I buy a handful of roses as I come up from the office, perhaps, and Prue arranges them so prettily in a glass dish for the centre of the table that even when I have hurried out to see Aurelia step into her carriage to go out to dine, I have thought that the bouquet she carried was not more beautiful because it was more costly. I grant that it was more harmonious with her superb beauty and her rich attire. And I have no doubt that if Aurelia knew the old man, whom she must have seen so often watching her, and his wife, who ornaments her sex with as much sweetness, although with less splendour, than Aurelia herself, she would also acknowledge that the nosegay of roses was as fine and fit upon their table as her own sumptuous bouquet is for herself. I have that faith in the perception of that lovely lady. It is at least my habit—I hope I may say, my nature, to believe the best of people, rather than the worst. If I thought that all this sparkling setting of beauty—this fine fashion—these blazing jewels and lustrous silks and airy gauzes, embellished with gold-threaded embroidery and wrought in a thousand exquisite elaborations, so that I cannot see one of those lovely girls pass me by without thanking God for the vision—if I thought that this was all, and that underneath her lace flounces and diamond bracelets Aurelia was a sullen, selfish woman, then I should turn sadly homewards, for I should see that her jewels were flashing scorn upon the object they adorned, and that her laces were of a more exquisite loveliness than the woman whom they merely touched with a superficial grace. It would be like a gaily decorated mausoleum—bright to see, but silent and dark within.

'Great excellences, my dear Prue,' I sometimes allow myself to say, 'lie concealed in the depths of character, like pearls at the bottom of the sea. Under the laughing, glancing surface, how little they are suspected! Perhaps love is nothing else than the sight of them by one person. Hence, every man's mistress is apt to be an enigma to everybody else. I have no doubt that when Aurelia is engaged, people will say that she is a most admirable girl, certainly; but they cannot understand why any man should be in love with her. As if it were at all necessary that they should! And her lover, like a boy who finds a pearl in the public street, and wonders as much that others did not see it as that he did, will tremble until he knows his passion is returned; feeling, of course, that the whole world must be in love with this paragon who cannot possibly smile upon anything so unworthy as he.'

'I hope, therefore, my dear Mrs Prue,' I continue to say

to my wife, who looks up from her work regarding me with pleased pride, as if I were such an irresistible humorist,' you will allow me to believe that the depth may be calm although the surface is dancing. If you tell me that Aurelia is but a giddy girl, I shall believe that you think so. But I shall know, all the while, what profound dignity, and sweetness, and peace lie at the foundation of her character.'

I say such things to Titbottom during the dull season at the office. And I have known him sometimes to reply with a kind of dry, sad humour, not as if he enjoyed the joke, but as if the joke must be made, that he saw no reason why I should be dull because the season was so.

'And what do I know of Aurelia or any other girl?' he says to me with that abstracted air. 'I, whose Aurelias were of another century and another zone.'

Then he falls into a silence, which it seems quite profane to interrupt. But as we sit upon our high stools at the desk opposite each other, I leaning upon my elbows and looking at him; he, with sidelong face, glancing out of the window, as if it commanded a boundless landscape, instead of a dim, dingy office court, I cannot refrain from saying:

'Well!'

He turns slowly, and I go chatting on—a little too loquacious, perhaps, about those young girls. But I know that Titbottom regards such an excess as venial, for his sadness is so sweet that you could believe it the reflection of a smile from long, long years ago.

One day, after I had been talking for a long time, and we had put up our books, and were preparing to leave, he stood for some time by the window, gazing with a drooping intentness, as if he really saw something more than the dark court, and said slowly:

'Perhaps you would have different impressions of things if you saw them through my spectacles.'

'There was no change in his expression. He still looked from the window, and I said:

'Titbottom, I did not know that you used glasses. I have never seen you wearing spectacles.'

'No, I don't often wear them. I am not very fond of looking through them. But sometimes an irresistible necessity compels me to put them on, and I cannot help seeing.' Titbottom sighed.

'Is it so grievous a fate, to see?' inquired I.

'Yes; through my spectacles,' he said, turning slowly and looking at me with wan solemnity.

It grew dark as we stood in the office talking, and taking our hats we went out together. The narrow street of business was deserted. The heavy iron shutters were gloomily closed over the windows. From one or two offices struggled the dim gleam of an early candle, by whose light some perplexed accountant sat belated, and hunting for his error. A careless clerk passed, whistling. But the great tide of life had ebbed. We heard its roar far away, and the sound stole into that silent street like the murmur of the ocean into an inland dell.

'You will come and dine with us, Titbottom?'

He assented by continuing to walk with me, and I think we were both glad when we reached the house, and Prue came to meet us, saying:

'Do you know I hoped you would bring Mr Titbottom to dine?'

Titbottom smiled gently, and answered:

'He might have brought his spectacles with him, and I have been a happier man for it.'

Prue looked a little puzzled.

'My dear,' I said, you must know that our friend, Mr Titbottom, is the happy possessor of a pair of wonderful spectacles. I have never seen them, indeed; and, from what he says, I should be rather afraid of being seen by them. Most short-sighted persons are very glad to have the help of glasses; but Mr Titbottom seems to find very little pleasure in his.'

'It is because they make him too far-sighted, perhaps,' interrupted Prue quietly, as she took the silver soup-ladle from the sideboard.

We sipped our wine after dinner, and Prue took to her work. Can a man be too far-sighted? I did not ask the question aloud. The very tone in which Prue had spoken convinced me that he might.

'At least,' I said, 'Mr Titbottom will not refuse to tell us the history of his mysterious spectacles. I have known plenty of magic in eyes'—and I glanced at the tender blue eyes of Prue—'but I have not heard of any enchanted glasses.'

'Yet you must have seen the glass in which your wife looks every morning, and I take it that glass must be daily enchanted.' said Titbottom, with a bow of quaint respect to my wife.

I do not think I have seen such a blush upon Prue's cheek since—well, since a great many years ago.

'I will gladly tell you the history of my spectacles,' began Titbottom. It is very simple; and I am not at all sure that a great many other people have not a pair of the same kind. I have never, indeed, heard of them by the gross, like those of our young friend, Moses, the son of the Vicar of Wakefield. In fact, I think a gross would be quite enough to supply the world. It is a kind of article for which the demand does not increase with use. If we should all wear spectacles like mine, we should never smile any more. Oh—I am not quite sure—we should all be very happy.'

'A very important difference,' said Prue, counting her stitches.

'You know my grandfather Titbottom was a West Indian. A large proprietor, and an easy man, he basked in the tropical sun, leading his quiet, luxurious life. He lived much alone, and was what people call eccentric, by which I understand that he was very much himself, and, refusing the influence of other people, they had their little revenges, and called him names. It is a habit not exclusively tropical. I think I have seen the same thing even in this city. But he was greatly beloved—my bland and bountiful grandfather. He was so large-hearted and open-handed. He was so friendly, and thoughtful, and genial, that even his jokes had the air of graceful benedictions. He did not seem to grow old, and he was one of those who never appear to have been very young. He flourished in a perennial maturity, an immortal middle-age.

'My grandfather lived upon one of the small islands, St. Kit's, perhaps, and his domain extended to the sea. His house, a rambling West Indian mansion, was surrounded with deep, spacious piazzas, covered with luxurious lounges, among which one capacious chair was his peculiar seat. They tell me he used sometimes to sit there for the whole day, his great, soft, brown eyes fastened upon the sea, watching the specks of sails that flashed upon the horizon, while the evanescent expressions chased each other over his placid face, as if it reflected the calm and changing sea before him. His morning costume was an ample dressing-gown of gorgeously flowered silk, and his morning was very apt to last all day.

'He rarely read, but he would pace the great piazza for

hours, with his hands sunken in the pockets of his dressing-gown, and an air of sweet reverie, which any author might be very happy to produce.

'Society, of course, he saw little. There was some slight apprehension that if he were bidden to social entertainments he might forget his coat, or arrive without some other essential part of his dress; and there is a sly tradition in the Titbottom family that, having been invited to a ball in honour of the new governor of the island, my grandfather Titbottom sauntered into the hall towards midnight, wrapped in the gorgeous flowers of his dressing-gown, and with his hands buried in the pockets, as usual. There was great excitement, and immense deprecation of gubernatorial ire. But it happened that the governor and my grandfather were old friends, and there was no offence. But as they were conversing together, one of the distressed managers cast indignant glances at the brilliant costume of my grandfather, who summoned him, and asked courteously:

'"Did you invite me or my coat?"

'"You, in a proper coat," replied the manager.

'The governor smiled approvingly, and looked at my grandfather.

'"My friend," said he to the manager, "I beg your pardon, I forgot."

'The next day my grandfather was seen promenading in full ball dress along the streets of the little town.

'"They ought to know," said he, "that I have a proper coat, and that not contempt nor poverty, but forgetfulness, sent me to a ball in my dressing-gown."

'He did not much frequent social festivals after this failure, but he always told the story with satisfaction and a quiet smile.

'To a stranger, life upon those little islands is uniform even to weariness. But the old native dons like my grandfather ripen in the prolonged sunshine, like the turtle upon the Bahama banks, nor know of existence more desirable. Life in the tropics I take to be a placid torpidity. During the long, warm mornings of nearly half a century, my grandfather Titbottom had sat in his dressing-gown and gazed at the sea. But one calm June day, as he slowly paced the piazza after breakfast, his dreamy glance was arrested by a little vessel, evidently nearing the shore. He called for his spyglass, and surveying the craft, saw that she came from the neighbouring island. She glided smoothly, slowly, over the summer sea. The warm morning air was sweet with perfumes, and silent with heat. The sea sparkled languidly, and the brilliant blue hung cloudlessly over. Scores of little island vessels had my grandfather seen come over the horizon, and cast anchor in the port. Hundreds of summer mornings had the white sails flashed and faded, like vague faces through forgotten dreams. But this time he laid down the spyglass, and leaned against a column of the piazza, and watched the vessel with an intentness that he could not explain. She came nearer and nearer, a graceful spectre in the dazzling morning.

'"Decidedly I must step down and see about that vessel," said my grandfather Titbottom.

'He gathered his ample dressing-gown about him, and stepped from the piazza with no other protection from the sun than the little smoking cap upon his head. His face wore a calm, beaming smile, as if he approved of all the world. He was not an old man, but there was almost a patriarchal pathos in his expression as he sauntered along in the sunshine towards the shore. A group of idle gazers was collected to watch the arrival. The little vessel furled her sails and drifted slowly landward, and as she was of very light draft, she came close to the shelving shore. A long plank was put out from her side, and the disembarkation commenced. My grandfather Titbottom stood looking on to see the passengers descend. There were but a few of them, and mostly traders from the neighbouring island. But suddenly the face of a young girl appeared over the side of the vessel, and she stepped upon the plank to descend. My grandfather Titbottom instantly advanced, and moving briskly reached the top of the plank at the same moment, and with the old tassel of his cap flashing in the sun, and one hand in the pocket of his dressing gown, with the other he handed the young lady carefully down the plank. That young lady was afterwards my grandmother Titbottom.

'And so, over the gleaming sea which he had watched so long, and which seemed thus to reward his patient gaze, came his bride that sunny morning.

'"Of course we are happy," he used to say: "For you are the gift of the sun I have loved so long and so well." And my grandfather Titbottom would lay his hand so tenderly upon the golden hair of his young bride, that you could fancy him a devout Parsee caressing sunbeams.

'There were endless festivities upon occasion of the marriage; and my grandfather did not go to one of them in his dressing-gown. The gentle sweetness of his wife melted every heart into love and sympathy. He was much older than she, without doubt. But age, as he used to say with a smile of immortal youth, is a matter of feeling, not of years. And if, sometimes, as she sat by his side upon the piazza, her fancy looked through her eyes upon that summer sea and saw a younger lover, perhaps some one of those graceful and glowing heroes who occupy the foreground of all young maidens' visions by the sea, yet she could not find one more generous and gracious, nor fancy one more worthy and loving than my grandfather Titbottom. And if in the moonlit midnight, while he lay calmly sleeping, she leaned out of the window and sank into vague reveries of sweet possibility, and watched the gleaming path of the moonlight upon the water, until the dawn glided over it—it was only that mood of nameless regret and longing, which underlies all human happiness—or it was the vision of that life of society, which she had never seen, but of which she had often read, and which looked very fair and alluring across the sea to a girlish imagination which knew that it should never know that reality.

'These West Indian years were the great days of the family,' said Titbottom, with an air of majestic and regal regret, pausing and musing in our little parlour, like a late Stuart in exile, remembering England. Prue raised her eyes from her work, and looked at him with a subdued admiration; for I have observed that, like the rest of her sex, she has a singular sympathy with the representative of a reduced family. Perhaps it is their finer perception, which leads these tender-hearted women to recognize the divine right of social superiority so much more readily than we; and yet, much as Titbottom was enhanced in my wife's admiration by the discovery that his dusky sadness of nature and expression was, as it were, the expiring gleam and late twilight of ancestral splendours, I doubt if Mr Bourne would have preferred him for bookkeeper a moment sooner upon that account. In truth, I have observed, downtown, that the fact of your ancestors doing nothing is not considered good proof that you can do anything. But Prue and her sex regard sentiment more than action, and I understand easily enough why she is never tired of hearing me read of Prince Charlie. If Titbottom had been only a little younger, a little handsomer, a little more gallantly dressed—in fact, a little more of the Prince

Charlie, I am sure her eyes would not have fallen again upon her work so tranquilly, as he resumed his story.

'I can remember my grandfather Titbottom, although I was a very young child, and he was a very old man. My young mother and my young grandmother are very distinct figures in my memory, ministering to the old gentleman, wrapped in his dressing-gown, and seated upon the piazza. I remember his white hair and his calm smile, and how, not long before he died, he called me to him, and laying his hand upon my head, said to me:

'"My child, the world is not this great sunny piazza, nor life the fairy stories which the women tell you here as you sit in their laps. I shall soon be gone, but I want to leave with you some memento of my love for you, and I know nothing more valuable than these spectacles, which your grandmother brought from her native island, when she arrived here one fine summer morning, long ago. I cannot quite tell whether, when you grow older, you will regard it as a gift of the greatest value or as something that you had been happier never to have possessed."

'"But grandpapa, I am not short-sighted."

'"My son, are you not human?" said the old gentleman; and how shall I ever forget the thoughtful sadness with which, at the same time he handed me the spectacles.

'Instinctively I put them on, and looked at my grandfather. But I saw no grandfather, no piazza, no flowered dressing-gown; I saw only a luxuriant palm tree, waving broadly over a tranquil landscape. Pleasant homes clustered around it. Gardens teeming with fruit and flowers; flocks quietly feeding; birds wheeling and chirping. I heard children's voices, and the low lullaby of happy mothers. The sound of cheerful singing came wafted from distant fields upon the light breeze. Golden harvests glistened out of sight, and I caught their rustling whisper of prosperity. A warm, mellow atmosphere bathed the whole. I have seen copies of the landscapes of the Italian painter Claude which seemed to me faint reminiscences of that calm and happy vision. But all this peace and prosperity seemed to flow from the spreading palm as from a fountain.

'I do not know how long I looked, but I had, apparently, no power, as I had no will, to remove the spectacles. What a wonderful island must Nevis be, thought I, if people carry such pictures in their pockets, only by buying a pair of spectacles! What wonder that my dear grandmother Titbottom has lived such a placid life, and has blessed us all with her sunny temper, when she has lived surrounded by such images of peace.

'My grandfather died. But still, in the warm morning sunshine upon the piazza, I felt his placid presence, and as I crawled into his great chair, and drifted on in reverie through the still, tropical day, it was as if his soft, dreamy eye had passed into my soul. My grandmother cherished his memory with tender regret. A violent passion of grief for his loss was no more possible than for the pensive decay of the year. We have no portrait of him, but I see always, when I remember him, that peaceful and luxuriant palm. And I think that to have known one good old man—one man who, through the chances and rubs of a long life, has carried his heart in his hand, like a palm branch, waving all discords into peace, helps our faith in God, in ourselves, and in each other, more than many sermons. I hardly know whether to be grateful to my grandfather for the spectacles; and yet when I remember that it is to them I owe the pleasant image of him which I cherish, I seem to myself sadly ungrateful.

'Madam,' said Titbottom to Prue, solemnly, 'my memory

is a long and gloomy gallery, and only remotely, at its further end, do I see the glimmer of soft sunshine, and only there are the pleasant pictures hung. They seem to me very happy along whose gallery the sunlight streams to their very feet, striking all the pictured walls into unfading splendour.'

Prue had laid her work in her lap, and as Titbottom paused a moment, and I turned towards her, I found her mild eyes fastened upon my face, and glistening with happy tears.

'Misfortunes of many kinds came heavily upon the family after the head was gone. The great house was relinquished. My parents were both dead, and my grandmother had entire charge of me. But from the moment that I received the gift of the spectacles, I could not resist their fascination, and I withdrew into myself, and became a solitary boy. There were not many companions for me of my own age, and they gradually left me, or, at least, had not a hearty sympathy with me; for if they teased me I pulled out my spectacles and surveyed them so seriously that they acquired a kind of awe of me, and evidently regarded my grandfather's gift as a concealed magical weapon, which might be dangerously drawn upon them at any moment. Whenever, in our games, there were quarrels and high words, and I began to feel about my dress and to wear a grave look, they all took the alarm, and shouted, "Look out for Titbottom's spectacles," and scattered like a flock of scared sheep.

'Nor could I wonder at it. For, at first, before they took the alarm, I saw strange sights when I looked at them through the glasses. If two were quarrelling about a marble or a ball, I had only to go behind a tree where I was concealed and look at them leisurely. Then the scene changed, and no longer a green meadow with boys playing, but a spot which I did not recognize, and forms that made me shudder or smile. It was not a big boy bullying a little one, but a young wolf with glistening teeth and a lamb cowering before him; or, it was a dog faithful and famishing—or a star going slowly into eclipse—or a rainbow fading—or a flower blooming—or a sun rising—or a waning moon. The revelations of the spectacles determined my feeling for the boys, and for all whom I saw through them. No shyness, nor awkwardness, nor silence, could separate me from those who looked lovely as lilies to my illuminated eyes. If I felt myself warmly drawn to anyone I struggled with the fierce desire of seeing him through the spectacles. I longed to enjoy the luxury of ignorant feeling, to love without knowing, to float like a leaf upon the eddies of life, drifted now to a sunny point, now to a solemn shade—now over glittering ripples, now over gleaming calms—and not to determined ports, a trim vessel with an inexorable rudder.

'But, sometimes, mastered after long struggles, I seized my spectacles and sauntered into the little town. Putting them to my eyes I peered into the houses and at the people who passed me. Here sat a family at breakfast, and I stood at the window looking in. O motley meal! Fantastic vision! The good mother saw her lord sitting opposite, a grave, respectable being, eating muffins. But I saw only a bank-bill, more or less crumpled and tattered, marked with a larger or lesser figure. If a sharp wind blew suddenly, I saw it tremble and flutter; it was thin, flat, impalpable. I removed my glasses, and looked with my eyes at the wife. I could have smiled to see the humid tenderness with which she regarded her strange vis-à-vis. Is life only a game of blind-man's-buff? Of droll cross-purposes?

'Or I put them on again, and looked at the wife. How many stout trees I saw—how many tender flowers—how many placid pools; yes, and how many little streams winding out of sight, shrinking before the large, hard, round eyes opposite, and slipping off into solitude and shade, with a low, inner song for their own solace. And in many houses I thought to see angels, nymphs, or at least, women, and could only find broomsticks, mops, or kettles, hurrying about, rattling, tinkling, in a state of shrill activity. I made calls upon elegant ladies, and after I had enjoyed the gloss of silk and the delicacy of lace, and the flash of jewels, I slipped on my spectacles, and saw a peacock's feather, flounced and furbelowed and fluttering; or an iron rod, thin, sharp, and hard; nor could I possibly mistake the movement of the drapery for any flexibility of the thing draped—or, mysteriously chilled, I saw a statue of perfect form, or flowing movement, it might be alabaster, or bronze, or marble—but sadly often it was ice; and I knew that after it had shone a little, and frozen a few eyes with its despairing perfection, it could not be put away in the niches of palaces for ornament and proud family tradition, like the alabaster, or bronze, or marble statues, but would melt, and shrink, and fall coldly away in colourless and useless water, be absorbed in the earth and utterly forgotten.

'But the true sadness was rather in seeing those who, not having the spectacles, thought that the iron rod was flexible, and the ice statue warm. I saw many a gallant heart, which seemed to me brave and loyal as the crusaders sent by genuine and noble faith to Syria and the sepulchre, pursuing, through days and nights, and a long life of devotion, the hope of lighting at least a smile in the cold eyes, if not a fire in the icy heart. I watched the earnest, enthusiastic sacrifice. I saw the pure resolve, the generous faith, the fine scorn of doubt, the impatience of suspicion. I watched the grace, the ardour, the glory of devotion. Through those strange spectacles how often I saw the noblest heart renouncing all other hope, all other ambition, all other life, than the possible love of some one of those statues. Ah! Me, it was terrible, but they had not the love to give. The Parian face was so polished and smooth, because there was no sorrow upon the heart—and, drearily often, no heart to be touched. I could not wonder that the noble heart of devotion was broken, for it had dashed itself against a stone. I wept, until my spectacles were dimmed for that hopeless sorrow; but there was a pang beyond tears for those icy statues.

'Still a boy, I was thus too much a man in knowledge—I did not comprehend the sights I was compelled to see. I used to tear my glasses away from my eyes, and, frightened at myself, run to escape my own consciousness. Reaching the small house where we then lived, I plunged into my grandmother's room and, throwing myself upon the floor, buried my face in her lap; and sobbed myself to sleep with premature grief. But when I awakened, and felt her cool hand upon my hot forehead, and heard the low, sweet song, or the gentle story, or the tenderly told parable from the Bible, with which she tried to soothe me, I could not resist the mystic fascination that lured me, as I lay in her lap, to steal a glance at her through the spectacles.

'Pictures of the Madonna have not her rare and pensive beauty. Upon the tranquil little islands her life had been eventless, and all the fine possibilities of her nature were like flowers that never bloomed. Placid were all her years; yet I have read of no heroine, of no woman great in sudden crises, that it did not seem to me she might have been. The wife and widow of a man who loved his own home better than the homes of others, I have yet heard of no queen, no belle, no imperial beauty, whom in grace, and brilliancy, and persuasive courtesy, she might not have surpassed.

'Madam,' said Titbottom to my wife, whose heart hung upon his story; 'your husband's young friend, Aurelia, wears sometimes a camelia in her hair, and no diamond in the ball-room seems so costly as that perfect flower, which women envy, and for whose least and withered petal men sigh; yet, in the tropical solitudes of Brazil, how many a camelia bud drops from a bush that no eye has ever seen, which, had it flowered and been noticed, would have gilded all hearts with its memory.

'When I stole these furtive glances at my grandmother, half fearing that they were wrong, I saw only a calm lake, whose shores were low, and over which the sky hung unbroken, so that the last star was clearly reflected. It had an atmosphere of solemn twilight tranquillity, and so completely did its unruffled surface blend with the cloudless, star-studded sky, that, when I looked through my spectacles at my grandmother, the vision seemed to me all heaven and stars. Yet, as I gazed and gazed, I felt what stately cities might well have been built upon those shores, and have flashed prosperity over the calm, like coruscations of pearls.

'I dreamed of gorgeous fleets, silken sailed and blown by perfumed winds, drifting over those depthless waters and through those spacious skies. I gazed upon the twilight, the inscrutable silence, like a God-fearing discoverer upon a new, and vast, and dim sea, bursting upon him through forest glooms, and in the fervour of whose impassioned gaze, a millennial and poetic world arises, and man need no longer die to be happy.

'My companions naturally deserted me, for I had grown wearily grave and abstracted: and, unable to resist the allurement of my spectacles, I was constantly lost in a world, of which those companions were part, yet of which they knew nothing. I grew cold and hard, almost morose; people seemed to me blind and unreasonable. They did the wrong thing. They called green, yellow; and black, white. Young men said of a girl, "What a lovely, simple creature!" I looked, and there was only a glistening wisp of straw, dry and hollow. Or they said, "What a cold, proud beauty!" I looked, and lo! A Madonna, whose heart held the world. Or they said, "What a wild, giddy girl!" and I saw a glancing, dancing mountain stream, pure as the virgin snows whence it flowed, singing through sun and shade, over pearls and gold dust, slipping along unstained by weed, or rain, or heavy foot of cattle, touching the flowers with a dewy kiss—a beam of grace, a happy song, a line of light, in the dim and troubled landscape.

'My grandmother sent me to school, but I looked at the master, and saw that he was a smooth, round ferule—or an improper noun—or a vulgar fraction, and refused to obey him. Or he was a piece of string, a rag, a willow-wand, and I had a contemptuous pity. But one was a well of cool, deep water, and looking suddenly in, one day, I saw the stars. He gave me all my schooling. With him I used to walk by the sea, and, as we strolled and the waves plunged in long legions before us, I looked at him through the spectacles, and as his eye dilated with the boundless view, and his chest heaved with an impossible desire, I saw Xerxes and his army tossing and glittering, rank upon rank, multitude upon multitude, out of sight, but ever regularly advancing and with the confused roar of ceaseless music, prostrating themselves in abject homage. Or, as with arms outstretched and hair streaming on the wind, he chanted full lines of the resounding *Iliad*, I saw Homer pacing the Aegean sands in the Greek sunsets of forgotten times.

'My grandmother died, and I was thrown into the world without resources, and with no capital but my spectacles. I tried to find employment, but men were shy of me. There was a vague suspicion that I was either a little crazed, or a good deal in league with the Prince of Darkness. My companions who would persist in calling a piece of painted muslin a fair and fragrant flower had no difficulty; success waited for them around every corner, and arrived in every ship. I tried to teach, for I loved children. But if anything excited my suspicion, and, putting on my spectacles, I saw that I was fondling a snake, or smelling at a bud with a worm in it, I sprang up in horror and ran away; or, if it seemed to me through the glasses that a cherub smiled upon me, or a rose was blooming in my buttonhole, then I felt myself imperfect and impure, not fit to be leading and training what was so essentially superior in quality to myself, and I kissed the children and left them weeping and wondering.

'In despair I went to a great merchant on the island, and asked him to employ me.

'"My young friend," said he, "I understand that you have some singular secret, some charm, or spell, or gift, or something, I don't know what, of which people are afraid. Now, you know, my dear," said the merchant, swelling up, and apparently prouder of his great stomach than of his large fortune, "I am not of that kind. I am not easily frightened. You may spare yourself the pain of trying to impose upon me. People who propose to come to time before I arrive, are accustomed to arise very early in the morning," said he, thrusting his thumbs in the armholes of his waistcoat, and spreading the fingers, like two fans, upon his bosom. "I think I have heard something of your secret. You have a pair of spectacles, I believe, that you value very much, because your grandmother brought them as a marriage portion to your grandfather. Now, if you think fit to sell me those spectacles, I will pay you the largest market price for glasses. What do you say?"

'I told him that I had not the slightest idea of selling my spectacles.

'"My young friend means to eat them, I suppose," said he with a contemptuous smile.

'I made no reply, but was turning to leave the office, when the merchant called after me—

'"My young friend, poor people should never suffer themselves to get into pets. Anger is an expensive luxury, in which only men of a certain income can indulge. A pair of spectacles and a hot temper are not the most promising capital for success in life, Master Titbottom."

'I said nothing, but put my hand upon the door to go out, when the merchant said more respectfully—

'"Well, you foolish boy, if you will not sell your spectacles, perhaps you will agree to sell the use of them to me. That is, you shall only put them on when I direct you, and for my purposes. Hallo! You little fool!" cried he impatiently, as he saw that I intended to make no reply.

'But I had pulled out my spectacles, and put them on for my own purpose, and against his direction and desire. I looked at him, and saw a huge bald-headed wild boar, with gross chops and a leering eye—only the more ridiculous for the high-arched, gold-bowed spectacles, that straddled his nose. One of his fore hoofs was thrust into the safe, where his bills payable were hived, and the other into his pocket, among the loose change and bills there. His ears were pricked forward with a brisk, sensitive smartness. In a world where prize pork was the best excellence, he would have carried off all the premiums.

'I stepped into the next office in the street, and a mild-faced, genial man, also a large and opulent merchant, asked me my business in such a tone, that I instantly looked through my spectacles, and saw a land flowing with milk and honey. There I pitched my tent, and stayed till the good man died, and his business was discontinued.

'But while there,' said Titbottom, and his voice trembled away into a sigh, 'I first saw Preciosa. Spite of the spectacles, I saw Preciosa. For days, for weeks, for months, I did not take my spectacles with me. I ran away from them, I threw them up on high shelves, I tried to make up my mind to throw them into the sea, or down the well. I could not, I would not, I dared not look at Preciosa through the spectacles. It was not possible for me deliberately to destroy them; but I awoke in the night, and could almost have cursed my dear old grandfather for his gift. I escaped from the office, and sat for whole days with Preciosa. I told her the strange things I had seen with my mystic glasses. The hours were not enough for the wild romances which I raved in her ear. She listened, astonished and appalled. Her blue eyes turned upon me with a sweet deprecation. She clung to me, and then withdrew, and fled fearfully from the room. But she could not stay away. She could not resist my voice, in whose tones burned all the love that filled my heart and brain. The very effort to resist the desire of seeing her as I saw everybody else, gave a frenzy and an unnatural tension to my feeling and my manner. I sat by her side, looking into her eyes, smoothing her hair, folding her to my heart, which was sunken and deep—why not forever?—in that dream of peace. I ran from her presence, and shouted, and leaped with joy, and sat the whole night through, thrilled into happiness by the thought of her love and loveliness, like a wind-harp, tightly strung, and answering the airiest sigh of the breeze with music. Then came calmer days—the conviction of deep love settled upon our lives—as after the hurrying, heaving days of spring, comes the bland and benignant summer.

'"It is no dream, then, after all, and we are happy," I said to her, one day; and there came no answer, for happiness is speechless.

'We are happy then,' I said to myself, 'there is no excitement now. How glad I am that I can now look at her through my spectacles.'

'I feared lest some instinct should warn me to beware. I escaped from her arms, and ran home and seized the glasses and bounded back again to Preciosa. As I entered the room I was heated, my head was swimming with confused apprehension, my eyes must have glared. Preciosa was frightened, and rising from her seat, stood with an inquiring glance of surprise in her eyes. But I was bent with frenzy upon my purpose. I was merely aware that she was in the room. I saw nothing else. I heard nothing. I cared for nothing, but to see her through that magic glass, and feel at once, all the fulness of blissful perfection which that would reveal. Preciosa stood before the mirror, but alarmed at my wild and eager movements, unable to distinguish what I had in my hands, and seeing me raise them suddenly to my face, she shrieked with terror, and fell fainting upon the floor, at the very moment that I placed the glasses before my eyes, and beheld—myself, reflected in the mirror, before which she had been standing.

'Dear madam,' cried Titbottom, to my wife, springing up and falling back again in his chair, pale and trembling, while Prue ran to him and took his hand, and I poured out a glass of water—'I saw myself.'

There was silence for many minutes. Prue laid her hand gently upon the head of our guest, whose eyes were closed, and who breathed softly, like an infant in sleeping. Perhaps, in all the long years of anguish since that hour, no tender hand had touched his brow, nor wiped away the damps of a bitter sorrow. Perhaps the tender, maternal fingers of my wife soothed his weary head with the conviction that he felt the hand of his mother playing with the long hair of her boy in the soft West Indian morning. Perhaps it was only the natural relief of expressing a pent-up sorrow. When he spoke again, it was with the old, subdued tone, and the air of quaint solemnity.

'These things were matters of long, long ago, and I came to this country soon after. I brought with me, premature age, a past of melancholy memories, and the magic spectacles. I had become their slave. I had nothing more to fear. Having seen myself, I was compelled to see others, properly to understand my relations to them. The lights that cheer the future of other men had gone out for me. My eyes were those of an exile turned backwards upon the receding shore, and not forwards with hope upon the ocean. I mingled with men, but with little pleasure. There are but many varieties of a few types. I did not find those I came to clearer sighted than those I had left behind. I heard men called shrewd and wise, and report said they were highly intelligent and successful. But when I looked at them through my glasses, I found no halo of real manliness. My finest sense detected no aroma of purity and principle; but I saw only a fungus that had fattened and spread in a night. They all went to the theatre to see actors upon the stage. I went to see actors in the boxes, so consummately cunning, that the others did not know they were acting, and they did not suspect it themselves.

'Perhaps you wonder it did not make me misanthropical. My dear friends, do not forget that I had seen myself. It made me compassionate, not cynical. Of course I could not value highly the ordinary standards of success and excellence. When

I went to church and saw a thin, blue, artificial flower, or a great sleepy cushion expounding the beauty of holiness to pews full of eagles, half-eagles, and threepences, however adroitly concealed in broadcloth and boots: or saw an onion in an Easter bonnet weeping over the sins of Magdalen, I did not feel as they felt who saw in all this, not only propriety, but piety. Or when at public meetings an eel stood up on end, and wriggled and squirmed lithely in every direction, and declared that, for his part, he went in for rainbows and hot water—how could I help seeing that he was still black and loved a slimy pool?

'I could not grow misanthropical when I saw in the eyes of so many who were called old, the gushing fountains of eternal youth, and the light of an immortal dawn, or when I saw those who were esteemed unsuccessful and aimless, ruling a fair realm of peace and plenty, either in themselves, or more perfectly in another—a realm and princely possession for which they had well renounced a hopeless search and a belated triumph. I knew one man who had been for years a by-word for having sought the philosopher's stone. But I looked at him through the spectacles and saw a satisfaction in concentrated energies, and a tenacity arising from devotion to a noble dream, which was not apparent in the youths who pitied him in the aimless effeminacy of clubs, nor in the clever gentlemen who cracked their thin jokes upon him over a gossiping dinner.

'And there was your neighbour over the way, who passes for a woman who has failed in her career, because she is an old maid. People wag solemn heads of pity, and say that she made so great a mistake in not marrying the brilliant and famous man who was for long years her suitor. It is clear that no orange flower will ever bloom for her. The young people make tender romances about her as they watch her, and think of her solitary hours of bitter regret, and wasting longing, never to be satisfied. When I first came to town I shared this sympathy, and pleased my imagination with fancying her hard struggle with the conviction that she had lost all that made life beautiful. I supposed that if I looked at her through my spectacles, I should see that it was only her radiant temper which so illuminated her dress, that we did not see it to be heavy sables. But when, one day, I did raise my glasses and glanced at her, I did not see the old maid whom we all pitied for a secret sorrow, but a woman whose nature was a tropic, in which the sun shone, and birds sang, and flowers bloomed forever. There were no regrets, no doubts and half wishes, but a calm sweetness, a transparent peace. I saw her blush when that old lover passed by, or paused to speak to her, but it was only the sign of delicate feminine consciousness. She knew his love, and honoured it, although she could not understand it nor return it. I looked closely at her, and I saw that although all the world had exclaimed at her indifference to such homage, and had declared it was astonishing she should lose so fine a match, she would only say simply and quietly—

'"If Shakespeare loved me and I did not love him, how could I marry him?"

'Could I be misanthropical when I saw such fidelity, and dignity, and simplicity?

'You may believe that I was especially curious to look at that old lover of hers, through my glasses. He was no longer young, you know, when I came, and his fame and fortune were secure. Certainly I have heard of few men more beloved, and of none more worthy to be loved. He had the easy manner of a man of the world, the sensitive grace of a poet, and the charitable judgement of a wide traveller. He was accounted the most successful and most unspoiled of men. Handsome, brilliant, wise, tender, graceful, accomplished, rich, and famous, I looked at him, without the spectacles, in surprise, and admiration, and wondered how your neighbour over the way had been so entirely untouched by his homage. I watched their intercourse in society, I saw her gay smile, her cordial greeting; I marked his frank address, his lofty courtesy. Their manner told no tales. The eager world was balked, and I pulled out my spectacles.

'I had seen her, already, and now I saw him. He lived only in memory, and his memory was a spacious and stately palace. But he did not oftenest frequent the banqueting hall, where were endless hospitality and feasting—nor did he loiter much in reception rooms, where a throng of new visitors was forever swarming—nor did he feed his vanity by haunting the apartment in which were stored the trophies of his varied triumphs—nor dream much in the great gallery hung with pictures of his travels. But from all these lofty halls of memory he constantly escaped to a remote and solitary chamber, into which no one had ever penetrated. But my fatal eyes, behind the glasses, followed and entered with him, and saw that the chamber was a chapel. It was dim, and silent, and sweet with perpetual incense that burned upon an altar before a picture forever veiled. There, whenever I chanced to look, I saw him kneel and pray; and there, by day and by night, a funeral hymn was chanted.

'I do not believe you will be surprised that I have been content to remain deputy book-keeper. My spectacles regulated my ambition, and I early learned that there were better gods than Plutus. The glasses have lost much of their fascination now, and I do not often use them. Sometimes the desire is irresistible. Whenever I am greatly interested, I am compelled to take them out and see what it is that I admire.

'And yet—and yet,' said Titbottom, after a pause, 'I am not

sure that I thank my grandfather.'

Prue had long since laid away her work, and had heard every word of the story. I saw that the dear woman had yet one question to ask, and had been earnestly hoping to hear something that would spare her the necessity of asking. But Titbottom had resumed his usual tone, after the momentary excitement, and made no further allusion to himself. We all sat silently; Titbottom's eyes fastened musingly upon the carpet: Prue looking wistfully at him, and I regarding both.

It was past midnight, and our guest arose to go. He shook hands quietly, made his grave Spanish bow to Prue, and taking his hat, went towards the front door. Prue and I accompanied him. I saw in her eyes that she would ask her question. And as Titbottom opened the door, I heard the low words:

'And Preciosa?'

Titbottom paused. He had just opened the door and the moonlight streamed over him as he stood, turning back to us.

'I have seen her but once since. It was in church, and she was kneeling with her eyes closed, so that she did not see me. But I rubbed the glasses well, and looked at her, and saw a white lily, whose stem was broken, but which was fresh; and luminous, and fragrant, still.'

'That was a miracle,' interrupted Prue.

'Madam, it was a miracle,' replied Titbottom, 'and for that one sight I am devoutly grateful for my grandfather's gift. I saw, that although a flower may have lost its hold upon earthly moisture, it may still bloom as sweetly, fed by the dews of heaven.'

The door closed, and he was gone. But as Prue put her arm in mine and we went upstairs together, she whispered in my ear:

'How glad I am that you don't wear spectacles.'

THE DEATH OF A GOVERNMENT CLERK

Anton Chekhov

One fine evening, a no less fine government clerk called Ivan Dmitritch Tchervyakov was sitting in the second row of the stalls, gazing through an opera glass at the *Cloches de Corneville*. He gazed and felt at the acme of bliss. But suddenly... in stories one so often meets with this 'But suddenly'. The authors are right: life is so full of surprises! But suddenly his face puckered up, his eyes disappeared, his breathing was arrested...he took the opera glass from his eyes, bent over and... 'Aptchee!' he sneezed as you perceive. It is not reprehensible for anyone to sneeze anywhere. Peasants sneeze and so do police superintendents, and sometimes even privy councillors. All men sneeze. Tchervyakov was not in the least confused, he wiped his face with his handkerchief, and like a polite man, looked round to see whether he had disturbed anyone by his sneezing. But then he was overcome with confusion. He saw that an old gentleman sitting in front of him in the first row of the stalls was carefully wiping his bald head and his neck with his glove and muttering something to himself. In the old gentleman, Tchervyakov recognized Brizzhalov, a civilian general serving in the Department of Transport.

'I have spattered him,' thought Tchervyakov, 'he is not the head of my department, but still it is awkward. I must apologize.'

Tchervyakov gave a cough, bent his whole person forward, and whispered in the general's ear.

'Pardon, your Excellency, I spattered you accidentally...'

'Never mind, never mind.'

'For goodness sake excuse me, I...I did not mean to.'

'Oh, please, sit down! Let me listen!'

Tchervyakov was embarrassed, he smiled stupidly and fell to gazing at the stage. He gazed at it but was no longer feeling bliss. He began to be troubled by uneasiness. In the interval, he went up to Brizzhalov, walked beside him, and overcoming his shyness, muttered:

'I spattered you, your Excellency, forgive me...you see...I didn't do it to...'

'Oh, that's enough...I'd forgotten it, and you keep on about it!' said the general, moving his lower lip impatiently.

'He has forgotten, but there is a fiendish light in his eye,' thought Tchervyakov, looking suspiciously at the general. 'And he doesn't want to talk. I ought to explain to him...that I really didn't intend...that it is the law of nature or else he will think I meant to spit on him. He doesn't think so now, but he will think so later!'

On getting home, Tchervyakov told his wife of his breach of good manners. It struck him that his wife took too frivolous a view of the incident; she was a little frightened, but when she learned that Brizzhalov was in a different department, she was reassured.

'Still, you had better go and apologize,' she said, 'or he will think you don't know how to behave in public.'

'That's just it! I did apologize, but he took it somehow queerly...he didn't say a word of sense. There wasn't time to talk properly.'

Next day Tchervyakov put on a new uniform, had his hair cut and went to Brizzhalov's to explain; going into the General's reception room he saw there a number of petitioners and among them the General himself, who was beginning to interview them. After questioning several petitioners the General raised his eyes and looked at Tchervyakov.

'Yesterday at the Arcadia, if you recollect, your Excellency,' the latter began, 'I sneezed and...accidentally spattered...Exc...'

'What nonsense... It's beyond anything! What can I do for you,' said the General addressing the next petitioner.

'He won't speak,' thought Tchervyakov, turning pale; 'that means that he is angry... No, it can't be left like this... I will explain to him.'

When the General had finished his conversation with the last of the petitioners and was turning towards his inner apartments, Tchervyakov took a step towards him and muttered:

'Your Excellency! If I venture to trouble your Excellency, it is simply from a feeling I may say of regret...! It was not intentional if you will graciously believe me.'

The General made a lachrymose face, and waved his hand.

'Why, you are simply making fun of me, sir,' he said as he closed the door behind him.

'Where's the making fun in it?' thought Tchervyakov, 'there is nothing of the sort! He is a general, but he can't understand. If that is how it is I am not going to apologize to that fanfaron any more! The devil take him. I'll write a letter to him, but I won't go. By Jove, I won't.'

So thought Tchervyakov as he walked home; he did not

write a letter to the General, he pondered and pondered and could not make up that letter. He had to go next day to explain in person.

'I ventured to disturb your Excellency yesterday,' he muttered, when the General lifted enquiring eyes upon him, 'not to make fun as you were pleased to say. I was apologizing for having spattered you in sneezing... And I did not dream of making fun of you. Should I dare to make fun of you, if we should take to making fun, then there would be no respect for persons, there would be...'

'Be off!' yelled the General, turning suddenly purple, and shaking all over.

'What?' asked Tchervyakov, in a whisper turning numb with horror.

'Be off!' repeated the General, stamping.

Something seemed to give way in Tchervyakov's stomach. Seeing nothing and hearing nothing he reeled to the door, went out into the street, and went staggering along... Reaching home mechanically, without taking off his uniform, he lay down on the sofa and died.

THE NOSE

Nikolai Gogol

I

On 25 March 18—, a very strange occurrence took place in St. Petersburg. On the Ascension Avenue there lived a barber of the name of Ivan Jakovlevitch. He had lost his family name, and on his sign-board, on which was depicted the head of a gentleman with one cheek soaped, the only inscription to be read was, 'Blood-letting done here.'

On this particular morning he awoke pretty early. Becoming aware of the smell of fresh-baked bread, he sat up a little in bed, and saw his wife, who had a special partiality for coffee, in the act of taking some fresh-baked bread out of the oven.

'Today, Prasskovna Ossipovna,' he said, 'I do not want any coffee; I should like a fresh loaf with onions.'

'The blockhead may eat bread only as far as I am concerned,' said his wife to herself, 'then I shall have a chance of getting some coffee.' And she threw a loaf on the table.

For the sake of propriety, Ivan Jakovlevitch drew a coat over his shirt, sat down at the table, shook out some salt for himself, prepared two onions, assumed a serious expression, and began to cut the bread. After he had cut the loaf in two halves, he looked, and to his great astonishment saw something whitish sticking in it. He carefully poked round it with his knife, and felt it with his finger.

'Quite firmly fixed!' he murmured in his beard. 'What can it be?'

He put in his finger, and drew out—a nose!

Ivan Jakovlevitch at first let his hands fall from sheer astonishment; then he rubbed his eyes and began to feel it. A nose, an actual nose; and, moreover, it seemed to be the nose of an acquaintance! Alarm and terror were depicted in Ivan's face; but these feelings were slight in comparison with the disgust which took possession of his wife.

'Whose nose have you cut off, you monster?' she screamed, her face red with anger. 'You scoundrel! You tippler! I myself will report you to the police! Such a rascal! Many customers have told me that while you were shaving them, you held them so tight by the nose that they could hardly sit still.'

But Ivan Jakovlevitch was more dead than alive; he saw at once that this nose could belong to no other than to Kovaloff, a member of the Municipal Committee whom he shaved every Sunday and Wednesday.

'Stop, Prasskovna Ossipovna! I will wrap it in a piece of cloth and place it in the corner. There it may remain for the present; later on I will take it away.'

'No, not there! Shall I endure an amputated nose in my room? You understand nothing except how to strop a razor. You know nothing of the duties and obligations of a respectable man. You vagabond! You good-for-nothing! Am I to undertake all responsibility for you at the police-office? Ah, you soap-smearer!

You blockhead! Take it away where you like, but don't let it stay under my eyes!'

Ivan Jakovlevitch stood there flabbergasted. He thought and thought, and knew not what he thought.

'The devil knows how that happened!' he said at last, scratching his head behind his ear. Whether I came home drunk last night or not, I really don't know; but in all probability this is a quite extraordinary occurrence, for a loaf is something baked and a nose is something different. I don't understand the matter at all.' And Ivan Jakovlevitch was silent. The thought that the police might find him in unlawful possession of a nose and arrest him, robbed him of all presence of mind. Already he began to have visions of a red collar with silver braid and of a sword—and he trembled all over.

At last he finished dressing himself, and to the accompaniment of the emphatic exhortations of his spouse, he wrapped up the nose in a cloth and issued into the street.

He intended to lose it somewhere—either at somebody's door, or in a public square, or in a narrow alley; but just then, in order to complete his bad luck, he was met by an acquaintance, who showered inquiries upon him. 'Hullo, Ivan Jakovlevitch! Whom are you going to shave so early in the morning?' etc., so that he could find no suitable opportunity to do what he wanted. Later on he did let the nose drop, but a sentry bore down upon him with his halberd, and said, 'Look out! You have let something drop!' and Ivan Jakovlevitch was obliged to pick it up and put it in his pocket.

A feeling of despair began to take possession of him; all the more as the streets became more thronged and the merchants began to open their shops. At last he resolved to go to the Isaac Bridge, where perhaps he might succeed in throwing it into the Neva.

But my conscience is a little uneasy that I have not yet given any detailed information about Ivan Jakovlevitch, an estimable man in many ways.

Like every honest Russian tradesman, Ivan Jakovlevitch was a terrible drunkard, and although he shaved other people's faces every day, his own was always unshaved. His coat (he never wore an overcoat) was quite mottled, i.e. it had been black, but become brownish-yellow; the collar was quite shiny, and instead of the three buttons, only the threads by which they had been fastened were to be seen.

Ivan Jakovlevitch was a great cynic, and when Kovaloff, the member of the Municipal Committee, said to him, as was his custom while being shaved, 'Your hands always smell, Ivan Jakovlevitch!' the latter asked, 'What do they smell of?' 'I don't know, my friend, but they smell very strong.' Ivan Jakovlevitch after taking a pinch of snuff would then, by way of reprisals, set to work to soap him on the cheek, the upper lip, behind the ears, on the chin, and everywhere.

This worthy man now stood on the Isaac Bridge. At first he looked round him, then he leant on the railings of the bridge, as though he wished to look down and see how many fish were swimming past, and secretly threw the nose, wrapped in a little piece of cloth, into the water. He felt as though a ton weight had been lifted off him, and laughed cheerfully. Instead, however, of going to shave any officials, he turned his steps to a building, the sign-board of which bore 'Tea served here', in order to have a glass of punch, when suddenly he perceived at the other end of the bridge a police inspector of imposing exterior, with long whiskers, three-cornered hat, and sword hanging at his side. He nearly fainted; but the police inspector beckoned to him with his hand and said, 'Come here, my dear sir.'

Ivan Jakovlevitch, knowing how a gentleman should behave, took his hat off quickly, went towards the police inspector and said, 'I hope you are in the best of health.'

'Never mind my health. Tell me, my friend, why you were standing on the bridge.'

'By heaven, gracious sir, I was on the way to my customers, and only looked down to see if the river was flowing quickly.'

'That is a lie! You won't get out of it like that. Confess the truth.'

'I am willing to shave Your Grace two or even three times a week gratis,' answered Ivan Jakovlevitch.

'No, my friend, don't put yourself out! Three barbers are busy with me already, and reckon it a high honour that I let them show me their skill. Now then, out with it! What were you doing there?'

Ivan Jakovlevitch grew pale. But here the strange episode vanishes in mist, and what further happened is not known.

II

Kovaloff, the member of the Municipal Committee, awoke fairly early that morning, and made a droning noise—'Brr! Brr!'— through his lips, as he always did, though he could not say why. He stretched himself, and told his valet to give him a little mirror which was on the table. He wished to look at the heat-boil which had appeared on his nose the previous evening; but to his great astonishment, he saw that instead of his nose he had a perfectly smooth vacancy in his face. Thoroughly alarmed, he ordered some water to be brought, and rubbed his eyes with a towel. Sure enough, he no longer had a nose! Then he sprang out of bed, and shook himself violently! No, no nose any more! He dressed himself and went at once to the police superintendent.

But before proceeding further, we must certainly give the reader some information about Kovaloff, so that he may know what sort of a man this member of the Municipal Committee really was. These committee-men, who obtain that title by means of certificates of learning, must not be compared with the committee-men appointed for the Caucasus district, who are of quite a different kind. The learned committee-man—but Russia is such a wonderful country that when one committee-man is spoken of all the others from Riga to Kamschatka refer it to themselves. The same is also true of all other titled officials. Kovaloff had been a Caucasian committee-man two years previously, and could not forget that he had occupied that position; but in order to enhance his own importance, he never called himself 'committee-man' but 'Major.'

'Listen, my dear,' he used to say when he met an old woman in the street who sold shirt-fronts,' go to my house in Sadovaia Street and ask "Does Major Kovaloff live here?" Any child can tell you where it is.'

Accordingly, we will call him in the future Major Kovaloff. It was his custom to take a daily walk on the Neffsky Avenue. The collar of his shirt was always remarkably clean and stiff. He wore the same style of whiskers as those that are worn by governors of districts, architects and regimental doctors; in short, all those who have full red cheeks and play a good game of whist. These whiskers grow straight across the cheek towards the nose.

Major Kovaloff wore a number of seals, on some of which were engraved armorial bearings, and others the names of the days of the week. He had come to St Petersburg with the view of obtaining some position corresponding to his rank, if possible that of vice-governor of a province; but he was prepared to be content with that of a bailiff in some department or other. He was, moreover, not disinclined to marry, but only such a lady who could bring with her a dowry of two hundred thousand roubles. Accordingly, the reader can judge for himself what his sensations were when he found in his face, instead of a fairly symmetrical nose, a broad, flat vacancy.

To increase his misfortune, not a single droshky was to be seen in the street, and so he was obliged to proceed on foot. He wrapped himself up in his cloak, and held his handkerchief to his face as though his nose bled. 'But perhaps it is all only my imagination; it is impossible that a nose should drop off in such a silly way,' he thought, and stepped into a confectioner's shop in order to look into the mirror.

Fortunately no customer was in the shop; only small shop-boys were cleaning it out, and putting chairs and tables straight. Others with sleepy faces were carrying fresh cakes on trays, and yesterday's newspapers stained with coffee were still lying about. 'Thank God no one is here!' he said to himself. 'Now I can look at myself leisurely.'

He stepped gingerly up to a mirror and looked.

'What an infernal face!' he exclaimed, and spat with disgust. 'If there were only something there instead of the nose, but there is absolutely nothing.'

He bit his lips with vexation, left the confectioner's, and resolved, quite contrary to his habit, neither to look nor smile at anyone on the street. Suddenly he halted as if rooted to the spot before a door, where something extraordinary happened. A carriage drew up at the entrance; the carriage door was opened, and a gentleman in uniform came out and hurried up the steps. How great was Kovaloff's terror and astonishment when he saw that it was his own nose!

At this extraordinary sight, everything seemed to turn round with him. He felt as though he could hardly keep upright on his legs; but, though trembling all over as though with fever, he resolved to wait till the nose should return to the carriage. After about two minutes the nose actually came out again. It wore a gold-embroidered uniform with a stiff, high collar, trousers of chamois leather, and a sword hung at its side. The hat, adorned with a plume, showed that it held the rank of a state-councillor. It was obvious that it was paying duty-calls. It looked round on both sides, called to the coachman 'Drive on,' and got into the carriage, which drove away.

Poor Kovaloff nearly lost his reason. He did not know what to think of this extraordinary procedure. And indeed how was it possible that the nose, which only yesterday he had on his face, and which could neither walk nor drive, should wear a uniform. He ran after the carriage, which fortunately had stopped a short way off before the Grand Bazar of Moscow. He hurried towards it and pressed through a crowd of beggar-women with their faces bound up, leaving only two openings for the eyes, over whom he had formerly so often made merry.

There were only a few people in front of the Bazar. Kovaloff was so agitated that he could decide on nothing, and looked for the nose everywhere. At last he saw it standing before a shop. It seemed half buried in its stiff collar, and was attentively inspecting the wares displayed.

'How can I get at it?' thought Kovaloff. 'Everything—the uniform, the hat, and so on—show that it is a state-councillor. How the deuce has that happened?'

He began to cough discreetly near it, but the nose paid him not the least attention.

'Honourable sir,' said Kovaloff at last, plucking up courage, 'honourable sir.'

'What do you want?' asked the nose, and turned round.

'It seems to me strange, most respected sir—you should know where you belong—and I find you all of a sudden—where? Judge yourself.'

'Pardon me, I do not understand what you are talking about. Explain yourself more distinctly.'

'How shall I make my meaning plainer to him?' Then plucking up fresh courage, he continued, 'Naturally—besides I am a Major. You must admit it is not befitting that I should go about without a nose. An old apple-woman on the Ascension Bridge may carry on her business without one, but since I am on the look out for a post; besides in many houses I am acquainted with ladies of high position—Madame Tchektyriev, wife of a state-councillor, and many others. So you see—I do not know, honourable sir, what you——' (here the Major shrugged his shoulders). 'Pardon me; if one regards the matter from the point of view of duty and honour—you will yourself understand——'

'I understand nothing,' answered the nose. I repeat, please explain yourself more distinctly.'

'Honourable sir,' said Kovaloff with dignity, 'I do not know how I am to understand your words. It seems to me the matter is as clear as possible. Or do you wish—but you are after all my own nose!'

The nose looked at the Major and wrinkled its forehead. 'There you are wrong, respected sir; I am myself. Besides, there can be no close relations between us. To judge by the buttons of your uniform, you must be in quite a different department to mine.' So saying, the nose turned away.

Kovaloff was completely puzzled; he did not know what to do, and still less what to think. At this moment he heard the pleasant rustling of a lady's dress, and there approached an elderly lady wearing a quantity of lace, and by her side her graceful daughter in a white dress which set off her slender figure to advantage, and wearing a light straw hat. Behind the ladies marched a tall lackey with long whiskers.

Kovaloff advanced a few steps, adjusted his cambric collar, arranged his seals which hung by a little gold chain, and with smiling face fixed his eyes on the graceful lady, who bowed lightly like a spring flower, and raised to her brow her little white hand with transparent fingers. He smiled still more when he spied under the brim of her hat her little round chin, and part of her cheek faintly tinted with rose-colour. But suddenly he sprang back as though he had been scorched. He remembered that he had nothing but an absolute blank in place of a nose, and tears started to his eyes. He turned round in order to tell the gentleman in uniform that he was only a state-councillor in appearance, but really a scoundrel and a rascal, and nothing else but his own nose; but the nose was no longer there. He had had time to go, doubtless in order to continue his visits.

His disappearance plunged Kovaloff into despair. He went back and stood for a moment under a colonnade, looking round him on all sides in hope of perceiving the nose somewhere. He remembered very well that it wore a hat with a plume in it and a gold-embroidered uniform; but he had not noticed the shape of the cloak, nor the colour of the carriages and the horses, nor even whether a lackey stood behind it, and, if so, what sort of livery he wore. Moreover, so many carriages were passing that it would have been difficult to recognize one, and even if he had done so, there would have been no means of stopping it.

The day was fine and sunny. An immense crowd was passing to and fro in the Neffsky Avenue; a variegated stream of ladies flowed along the pavement. There was his acquaintance, the Privy Councillor, whom he was accustomed to style 'General,' especially when strangers were present. There was Iarygin, his intimate friend who always lost in the evenings at whist; and there another Major, who had obtained the rank of committee-man in the Caucasus, beckoned to him.

'Go to the deuce!' said Kovaloff sotto voce. 'Hi! Coachman, drive me straight to the superintendent of police.' So saying, he got into a droshky and continued to shout all the time to the coachman 'Drive hard!'

'Is the police superintendent at home?' he asked on entering the front hall.

'No, sir,' answered the porter, 'he has just gone out.'

'Ah, just as I thought!'

'Yes,' continued the porter, he has only just out, 'if you had been a moment earlier you would perhaps have caught him.'

Kovaloff, still holding his handkerchief to his face, re-entered the droshky and cried in a despairing voice 'Drive on!'

'Where?' asked the coachman.

'Straight on!'

'But how? There are crossroads here. Shall I go to the right or the left?'

This question made Kovaloff reflect. In his situation it was necessary to have recourse to the police; not because the affair had anything to do with them directly but because they acted more promptly than other authorities. As for demanding any explanation from the department to which the nose claimed to belong, it would, he felt, be useless, for the answers of that gentleman showed that he regarded nothing as sacred, and he might just as likely have lied in this matter as in saying that he had never seen Kovaloff.

But just as he was about to order the coachman to drive to the police-station, the idea occurred to him that this rascally scoundrel who, at their first meeting, had behaved so disloyally towards him, might, profiting by the delay, quit the city secretly; and then all his searching would be in vain, or might last over a whole month. Finally, as though visited with a heavenly inspiration, he resolved to go directly to an advertisement office, and to advertise the loss of his nose, giving all its distinctive characteristics in detail, so that anyone who found it might bring it at once to him, or at any rate inform him where it lived. Having decided on this course, he ordered the coachman to drive to the advertisement office, and all the way he continued to punch him in the back—'Quick, scoundrel! quick!'

'Yes, sir!' answered the coachman, lashing his shaggy horse with the reins.

At last they arrived, and Kovaloff, out of breath, rushed into a little room where a grey-haired official, in an old coat and with spectacles on his nose, sat at a table holding his pen between his teeth, counting a heap of copper coins.

'Who takes in the advertisements here?' exclaimed Kovaloff.

'At your service, sir,' answered the grey-haired functionary, looking up and then fastening his eyes again on the heap of coins before him.

'I wish to place an advertisement in your paper—'

'Have the kindness to wait a minute,' answered the official, putting down figures on paper with one hand, and with the other moving two balls on his calculating-frame.

A lackey, whose silver-laced coat showed that he served in

one of the houses of the nobility, was standing by the table with a note in his hand, and speaking in a lively tone, by way of showing himself sociable. 'Would you believe it, sir, this little dog is really not worth twenty-four kopecks, and for my own part I would not give a farthing for it; but the countess is quite gone upon it, and offers a hundred roubles' reward to anyone who finds it. To tell you the truth, the tastes of these people are very different from ours; they don't mind giving five hundred or a thousand roubles for a poodle or a pointer, provided it be a good one.'

The official listened with a serious air while counting the number of letters contained in the note. At either side of the table stood a number of housekeepers, clerks and porters, carrying notes. The writer of one wished to sell a barouche, which had been brought from Paris in 1814 and had been very little used; others wanted to dispose of a strong droshky which wanted one spring, a spirited horse seventeen years old, and so on. The room where these people were collected was very small, and the air was very close; but Kovaloff was not affected by it, for he had covered his face with a handkerchief, and because his nose itself was heaven knew where.

'Sir, allow me to ask you—I am in a great hurry,' he said at last impatiently.

'In a moment! In a moment! Two roubles, twenty-four kopecks—one minute! One rouble, sixty-four kopecks!' said the grey-haired official, throwing their notes back to the housekeepers and porters. 'What do you wish?' he said, turning to Kovaloff.

'I wish—' answered the latter, 'I have just been swindled and cheated, and I cannot get hold of the perpetrator. I only want you to insert an advertisement to say that whoever brings this scoundrel to me will be well rewarded.'

'What is your name, please?'

'Why do you want my name? I have many lady friends— Madame Tchektyriev, wife of a state-councillor, Madame Podtotchina, wife of a Colonel. Heaven forbid that they should get to hear of it. You can simply write "committee-man," or, better, "Major".'

'And the man who has run away is your serf.'

'Serf! If he was, it would not be such a great swindle! It is the nose which has absconded.'

'H'm! What a strange name. And this Mr Nose has stolen from you a considerable sum?'

'Mr Nose! Ah, you don't understand me! It is my own nose which has gone, I don't know where. The devil has played a trick on me.'

'How has it disappeared? I don't understand.'

'I can't tell you how, but the important point is that now it walks about the city itself a state-councillor. That is why I want you to advertise that whoever gets hold of it should bring it as soon as possible to me. Consider; how can I live without such a prominent part of my body? It is not as if it were merely a little toe; I would only have to put my foot in my boot and no one would notice its absence. Every Thursday I call on the wife of M. Tchektyriev, the state-councillor; Madame Podtotchina, a Colonel's wife who has a very pretty daughter, is one of my acquaintances; and what am I to do now? I cannot appear before them like this.'

'The official compressed his lips and reflected. No, I cannot insert an advertisement like that,' he said after a long pause.

'What! Why not?'

'Because it might compromise the paper. Suppose everyone

could advertise that his nose was lost. People already say that all sorts of nonsense and lies are inserted.'

'But this is not nonsense! There is nothing of that sort in my case.'

'You think so? Listen a minute. Last week there was a case very like it. An official came, just as you have done, bringing an advertisement for the insertion of which he paid two roubles, sixty-three kopecks; and this advertisement simply announced the loss of a black-haired poodle. There did not seem to be anything out of the way in it, but it was really a satire; by the poodle was meant the cashier of some establishment or other.'

'But I am not talking of a poodle, but my own nose; that is almost myself.'

'No, I cannot insert your advertisement.'

'But my nose really has disappeared!'

'That is a matter for a doctor. There are said to be people who can provide you with any kind of nose you like. But I see that you are a witty man, and like to have your little joke.'

'But I swear to you on my word of honour. Look at my face yourself.'

'Why put yourself out?' continued the official, taking a pinch of snuff. 'All the same, if you don't mind,' he added with a touch of curiosity, 'I should like to have a look at it.'

The committee-man removed the handkerchief from before his face.

'It certainly does look odd,' said the official. It is perfectly flat like a freshly fried pancake. It is hardly credible.'

'Very well. Are you going to hesitate any more? You see it is impossible to refuse to advertise my loss. I shall be particularly obliged to you, and I shall be glad that this incident has procured me the pleasure of making your acquaintance.' The Major, we see, did not even shrink from a slight humiliation.

'It certainly is not difficult to advertise it,' replied the official, 'but I don't see what good it would do you. However, if you lay so much stress on it, you should apply to someone who has a skilful pen, so that he may describe it as a curious, natural freak, and publish the article in *The Northern Bee* (here he took another pinch) for the "benefit of youthful readers" (he wiped his nose), or simply as a matter worthy of "arousing public curiosity".'

The committee-man felt completely discouraged. He let his eyes fall absent-mindedly on a daily paper in which theatrical performances were advertised. Reading there the name of an actress whom he knew to be pretty, he involuntarily smiled, and his hand sought his pocket to see if he had a blue ticket—for in Kovaloff's opinion superior officers like himself should not take a lesser-priced seat; but the thought of his lost nose suddenly spoilt everything.

The official himself seemed touched at his difficult position. Desiring to console him, he tried to express his sympathy by a few polite words. 'I much regret,' he said, 'your extraordinary mishap. Will you not try a pinch of snuff? It clears the head, banishes depression, and is a good preventive against hæmorrhoids.'

So saying, he reached his snuff-box out to Kovaloff, skilfully concealing at the same time the cover, which was adorned with the portrait of some lady or other.

This act, quite innocent in itself, exasperated Kovaloff. 'I don't understand what you find to joke about in the matter,' he exclaimed angrily. 'Don't you see that I lack precisely the essential feature for taking snuff? The devil take your snuff-box. I don't want to look at snuff now, not even the best, certainly not your vile stuff!'

So saying, he left the advertisement office in a state of profound irritation, and went to the commissary of police. He arrived just as this dignitary was reclining on his couch, and saying to himself with a sigh of satisfaction, 'Yes, I shall make a nice little sum out of that.'

It might be expected, therefore, that the committee-man's visit would be quite inopportune.

This police commissary was a great patron of all the arts and industries; but what he liked above everything else was a cheque. 'It is a thing,' he used to say, to which it is not easy to find an equivalent; it requires no food, it does not take up much room, it stays in one's pocket, and if it falls, it is not broken.'

The commissary accorded Kovaloff a fairly frigid reception, saying that the afternoon was not the best time to come with a case, that nature required one to rest a little after eating (this showed the committee-man that the commissary was acquainted with the aphorisms of the ancient sages), and that respectable people did not have their noses stolen.

The last allusion was too direct. We must remember that Kovaloff was a very sensitive man. He did not mind anything said against him as an individual, but he could not endure any reflection on his rank or social position. He even believed that in comedies one might allow attacks on junior officers, but never on their seniors.

The commissary's reception of him hurt his feelings so much that he raised his head proudly, and said with dignity, 'After such insulting expressions on your part, I have nothing more to say.' And he left the place.

He reached his house quite wearied out. It was already growing dark. After all his fruitless search, his room seemed to him melancholy and even ugly. In the vestibule he saw his valet Ivan stretched on the leather couch and amusing himself by spitting at the ceiling, which he did very cleverly, hitting every time the same spot. His servant's equanimity enraged him; he struck him on the forehead with his hat, and said, 'You good-for-nothing, you are always playing the fool!'

Ivan rose quickly and hastened to take off his master's cloak.

Once in his room, the Major, tired and depressed, threw himself in an armchair and, after sighing a while, began to soliloquize:

'In heaven's name, why should such a misfortune befall me? If I had lost an arm or a leg, it would be less insupportable; but a man without a nose! Devil take it!—What is he good for? He is only fit to be thrown out of the window. If it had been taken from me in war or in a duel, or if I had lost it by my own fault! But it has disappeared inexplicably. But no! it is impossible,' he continued after reflecting a few moments, it is incredible that a nose can disappear like that—quite incredible. I must be dreaming, or suffering from some hallucination; perhaps I swallowed, by mistake instead of water, the brandy with which I rub my chin after being shaved. That fool of an Ivan must have forgotten to take it away, and I must have swallowed it.'

In order to find out whether he were really drunk, the Major pinched himself so hard that he unvoluntarily uttered a cry. The pain convinced him that he was quite wide awake. He walked slowly to the looking-glass and at first closed his eyes, hoping to see his nose suddenly in its proper place; but on opening them, he started back. 'What a hideous sight!' he exclaimed.

It was really incomprehensible. One might easily lose a button, a silver spoon, a watch, or something similar; but a loss like this, and in one's own dwelling!

After considering all the circumstances, Major Kovaloff felt inclined to suppose that the cause of all his trouble should be laid at the door of Madame Podtotchina, the Colonel's wife, who wished him to marry her daughter. He himself paid her court readily, but always avoided coming to the point. And when the lady one day told him point-blank that she wished him to marry her daughter, he gently drew back, declaring that he was still too young, and that he had to serve five years more before he would be forty-two. This must be the reason why the lady, in revenge, had resolved to bring him into disgrace, and had hired two sorceresses for that object. One thing was certain—his nose had not been cut off; no one had entered his room, and as for Ivan Jakovlevitch—he had been shaved by him on Wednesday, and during that day and the whole of Thursday his nose had been there, as he knew and well remembered. Moreover, if his nose had been cut off he would naturally have felt pain, and doubtless the wound would not have healed so quickly, nor would the surface have been as flat as a pancake.

All kinds of plans passed through his head: should he bring a legal action against the wife of a superior officer, or should he go to her and charge her openly with her treachery?

His reflections were interrupted by a sudden light, which shone through all the chinks of the door, showing that Ivan had lit the wax-candles in the vestibule. Soon Ivan himself came in with the lights. Kovaloff quickly seized a handkerchief and covered the place where his nose had been the evening before, so that his blockhead of a servant might not gape with his mouth wide open when he saw his master's extraordinary appearance.

Scarcely had Ivan returned to the vestibule than a stranger's voice was heard there.

'Does Major Kovaloff live here?' it asked.

'Come in!' said the Major, rising rapidly and opening the door.

He saw a police official of pleasant appearance, with grey whiskers and fairly full cheeks—the same who at the commencement of this story was standing at the end of the Isaac Bridge. 'You have lost your nose?' he asked.

'Exactly so.'

'It has just been found.'

'What—do you say?' stammered Major Kovaloff.

Joy had suddenly paralysed his tongue. He stared at the police commissary on whose cheeks and full lips fell the flickering light of the candle.

'How was it?' he asked at last.

By a very singular chance. It has been arrested just as it was getting into a carriage for Riga. Its passport had been made out some time ago in the name of an official; and what is still more strange, I myself took it at first for a gentleman. Fortunately I had my glasses with me, and then I saw at once that it was a nose. I am short-sighted, you know, and as you stand before me I cannot distinguish your nose, your beard, or anything else. My mother-in-law can hardly see at all.'

Kovaloff was beside himself with excitement. 'Where is it? Where? I will hasten there at once.'

'Don't put yourself out. Knowing that you need it, I have brought it with me. Another singular thing is that the principal culprit in the matter is a scoundrel of a barber living in the Ascension Avenue, who is now safely locked up. I had long suspected him of drunkenness and theft; only the day before yesterday he stole some buttons in a shop. Your nose is quite uninjured.' So saying, the police commissary put his hand in his pocket and brought out the nose wrapped up in paper.

'Yes, yes, that is it!' exclaimed Kovaloff. Will you not stay and drink a cup of tea with me?'

'I should like to very much, but I cannot. I must go at once to the House of Correction. The cost of living is very high nowadays. My mother-in-law lives with me, and there are several children; the eldest is very hopeful and intelligent, but I have no means for their education.'

After the commissary's departure, Kovaloff remained for some time plunged in a kind of vague reverie, and did not recover full consciousness for several moments, so great was the effect of this unexpected good news. He placed the recovered nose carefully in the palm of his hand, and examined it again with the greatest attention.

'Yes, this is it!' he said to himself. 'Here is the heat-boil on the left side, which came out yesterday.' And he nearly laughed aloud with delight.

But nothing is permanent in this world. Joy in the second moment of its arrival is already less keen than in the first, is still fainter in the third, and finishes by coalescing with our normal mental state, just as the circles which the fall of a pebble forms on the surface of water, gradually die away. Kovaloff began to meditate, and saw that his difficulties were not yet over; his nose had been recovered, but it had to be joined on again in its proper place.

And suppose it could not? As he put this question to himself, Kovaloff grew pale. With a feeling of indescribable dread, he rushed towards his dressing-table, and stood before the mirror in order that he might not place his nose crookedly. His hands trembled.

Very carefully he placed it where it had been before. Horror! It did not remain there. He held it to his mouth and warmed it a little with his breath, and then placed it there again; but it would not hold.

'Hold on, you stupid!' he said.

But the nose seemed to be made of wood, and fell back on the table with a strange noise, as though it had been a cork. The Major's face began to twitch feverishly. 'Is it possible that it won't stick?' he asked himself, full of alarm. But however often he tried, all his efforts were in vain.

He called Ivan, and sent him to fetch the doctor who occupied the finest flat in the mansion. This doctor was a man of imposing appearance, who had magnificent black whiskers and a healthy wife. He ate fresh apples every morning, and cleaned his teeth with extreme care, using five different toothbrushes for three-quarters of an hour daily.

The doctor came immediately. After having asked the Major when this misfortune had happened, he raised his chin and gave him a fillip with his finger just where the nose had been, in such a way that the Major suddenly threw back his head and struck the wall with it. The doctor said that did not matter; then, making him turn his face to the right, he felt the vacant place and said 'H'm!' then he made him turn it to the left and did the same; finally he again gave him a fillip with his finger, so that the Major stared like a horse whose teeth are being examined. After this experiment, the doctor shook his head and said, 'No, it cannot be done. Rather remain as you are, lest something worse happen. Certainly one could replace it at once, but I assure you the remedy would be worse than the disease.'

'All very fine, but how am I to go on without a nose?' answered Kovaloff. There is nothing worse than that. How can I show myself with such a villainous appearance? I go into good society, and this evening I am invited to two parties. I know several ladies, Madame Tchektyriev, the wife of a state-councillor, Madame Podtotchina—although after what she has done, I don't want to have anything to do with her except through the agency of the police. I beg you,' continued Kovaloff in a supplicating tone, 'find some way or other of replacing it; even if it is not quite firm, as long as it holds at all; I can keep it in place sometimes with my hand, whenever there is any risk. Besides, I do not even dance, so that it is not likely to be injured by any sudden movement. As to your fee, be in no anxiety about that; I can well afford it.'

'Believe me,' answered the doctor in a voice which was neither too high nor too low, but soft and almost magnetic, 'I do not treat patients from love of gain. That would be contrary to my principles and to my art. It is true that I accept fees, but that is only not to hurt my patients' feelings by refusing them. I could certainly replace your nose, but I assure you on my word of honour, it would only make matters worse. Rather let Nature do her own work. Wash the place often with cold water, and I assure you that even without a nose, you will be just as well as if you had one. As to the nose itself, I advise you to have it preserved in a bottle of spirits, or, still better, of warm vinegar mixed with two spoonfuls of brandy, and then you can sell it at a good price. I would be willing to take it myself, provided you do not ask too much.'

'No, no, I shall not sell it at any price. I would rather it were lost again.'

'Excuse me,' said the doctor, taking his leave. 'I hoped to be useful to you, but I can do nothing more; you are at any rate convinced of my goodwill.' So saying, the doctor left the room with a dignified air.

Kovaloff did not even notice his departure. Absorbed in a

profound reverie, he only saw the edge of his snow-white cuffs emerging from the sleeves of his black coat.

The next day he resolved, before bringing a formal action, to write to the Colonel's wife and see whether she would not return to him, without further dispute, that of which she had deprived him.

The letter ran as follows:

'To Madame Alexandra Podtotchina,

I hardly understand your method of action. Be sure that by adopting such a course you will gain nothing, and will certainly not succeed in making me marry your daughter. Believe me, the story of my nose has become well known; it is you and no one else who have taken the principal part in it. Its unexpected separation from the place which it occupied, its flight and its appearances sometimes in the disguise of an official, sometimes in proper person, are nothing but the consequence of unholy spells employed by you or by persons who, like you, are addicted to such honourable pursuits. On my part, I wish to inform you, that if the above-mentioned nose is not restored today to its proper place, I shall be obliged to have recourse to legal procedure.

For the rest, with all respect, I have the honour to be your humble servant,

Platon Kovaloff.'

The reply was not long in coming, and was as follows:

'Major Platon Kovaloff,

Your letter has profoundly astonished me. I must confess

that I had not expected such unjust reproaches on your part. I assure you that the official of whom you speak has not been at my house, either disguised or in his proper person. It is true that Philippe Ivanovitch Potantchikoff has paid visits at my house, and though he has actually asked for my daughter's hand, and was a man of good breeding, respectable and intelligent, I never gave him any hope. Again, you say something about a nose. If you intend to imply by that that I wished to snub you, i.e. to meet you with a refusal, I am very astonished because, as you well know, I was quite of the opposite mind. If after this you wish to ask for my daughter's hand, I should be glad to gratify you, for such has also been the object of my most fervent desire, in the hope of the accomplishment of which, I remain, yours most sincerely,

Alexandra Podtotchina.'

'No,' said Kovaloff, after having reperused the letter, 'she is certainly not guilty. It is impossible. Such a letter could not be written by a criminal.' The committee-man was experienced in such matters, for he had been often officially deputed to conduct criminal investigations while in the Caucasus. 'But then how and by what trick of fate has the thing happened?' he said to himself with a gesture of discouragement. 'The devil must be at the bottom of it.'

Meanwhile, the rumour of this extraordinary event had spread all over the city, and, as is generally the case, not without numerous additions. At that period there was a general disposition to believe in the miraculous; the public had recently been impressed by experiments in magnetism. The story of the floating chairs in Koniouchennaia Street was still quite recent, and there was nothing astonishing in hearing soon afterwards that Major Kovaloff's nose was to be seen walking every day at three o'clock on the Neffsky Avenue. The crowd of curious spectators which gathered there daily was enormous. On one occasion someone spread a report that the nose was in Junker's stores and immediately the place was besieged by such a crowd that the police had to interfere and establish order. A certain speculator with a grave, whiskered face, who sold cakes at a theatre door, had some strong wooden benches made which he placed before the window of the stores, and obligingly invited the public to stand on them and look in, at the modest charge of twenty-four kopecks. A veteran colonel, leaving his house earlier than usual expressly for the purpose, had the greatest difficulty in elbowing his way through the crowd, but to his great indignation he saw nothing in the store window but an ordinary flannel waistcoat and a coloured lithograph representing a young girl darning a stocking, while an elegant youth in a waistcoat with large lappels watched her from behind a tree. The picture had hung in the same place for more than ten years. The colonel went off, growling savagely to himself, 'How can the fools let themselves be excited by such idiotic stories?'

Then another rumour got abroad, to the effect that the nose of Major Kovaloff was in the habit of walking not on the Neffsky Avenue but in the Tauris Gardens. Some students of the Academy of Surgery went there on purpose to see it. A high-born lady wrote to the keeper of the gardens asking him to show her children this rare phenomenon, and to give them some suitable instruction on the occasion.

All these incidents were eagerly collected by the town wits, who just then were very short of anecdotes adapted to amuse ladies. On the other hand, the minority of solid, sober people were very much displeased. One gentleman asserted with great indignation that he could not understand how in our enlightened age such absurdities could spread abroad, and he was astonished that the Government did not direct their attention to the matter. This gentleman evidently belonged to the category of those people who wish the Government to interfere in everything, even in their daily quarrels with their wives.

But here the course of events is again obscured by a veil.

III

Strange events happen in this world, events which are sometimes entirely improbable. The same nose which had masqueraded as a state-councillor, and caused so much sensation in the town, was found one morning in its proper place, i.e. between the cheeks of Major Kovaloff, as if nothing had happened.

This occurred on 7 April. On awaking, the Major looked by chance into a mirror and perceived a nose. He quickly put his hand to it; it was there beyond a doubt!

'Oh!' exclaimed Kovaloff. For sheer joy he was on the point of performing a dance barefooted across his room, but the entrance of Ivan prevented him. He told him to bring water, and after washing himself, he looked again in the glass. The nose was there! Then he dried his face with a towel and looked again. Yes, there was no mistake about it!

'Look here, Ivan, it seems to me that I have a heat-boil on my nose,' he said to his valet.

And he thought to himself at the same time, 'That will be a nice business if Ivan says to me "No, sir, not only is there no boil, but your nose itself is not there!"'

But Ivan answered, 'There is nothing, sir; I can see no boil on your nose.'

'Good! Good!' exclaimed the Major, and snapped his fingers with delight.

At this moment the barber, Ivan Jakovlevitch, put his head in at the door, but as timidly as a cat which has just been beaten for stealing lard.

'Tell me first, are your hands clean?' asked Kovaloff when he saw him.

'Yes, sir.'

'You lie.'

'I swear they are perfectly clean, sir.'

'Very well; then come here.'

Kovaloff seated himself. Jakovlevitch tied a napkin under his chin, and in the twinkling of an eye covered his beard and part of his cheeks with a copious creamy lather.

'There it is!' said the barber to himself, as he glanced at the nose. Then he bent his head a little and examined it from one side. 'Yes, it actually is the nose—really, when one thinks——' he continued, pursuing his mental soliloquy and still looking at it. Then quite gently, with infinite precaution, he raised two fingers in the air in order to take hold of it by the extremity, as he was accustomed to do.

'Now then, take care!' Kovaloff exclaimed.

Ivan Jakovlevitch let his arm fall and felt more embarrassed than he had ever done in his life. At last he began to pass the razor very lightly over the Major's chin, and although it was very difficult to shave him without using the olfactory organ as a point of support, he succeeded, however, by placing his wrinkled thumb against the Major's lower jaw and cheek, thus overcoming all obstacles and bringing his task to a safe conclusion.

When the barber had finished, Kovaloff hastened to dress

himself, took a droshky, and drove straight to the confectioner's. As he entered it, he ordered a cup of chocolate. He then stepped straight to the mirror; the nose was there!

He returned joyfully, and regarded with a satirical expression two officers who were in the shop, one of whom possessed a nose not much larger than a waistcoat button.

After that he went to the office of the department where he had applied for the post of vice-governor of a province or Government bailiff. As he passed through the hall of reception, he cast a glance at the mirror; the nose was there! Then he went to pay a visit to another committee-man, a very sarcastic personage, to whom he was accustomed to say in answer to his raillery, 'Yes, I know, you are the funniest fellow in St Petersburg.'

On the way he said to himself, 'If the Major does not burst into laughter at the sight of me, that is a most certain sign that everything is in its accustomed place.'

But the Major said nothing. 'Very good!' thought Kovaloff.

As he returned, he met Madame Podtotchina with her daughter. He accosted them, and they responded very graciously. The conversation lasted a long time, during which he took more than one pinch of snuff, saying to himself, 'No, you haven't caught me yet, coquettes that you are! And as to the daughter, I shan't marry her at all.'

After that, the Major resumed his walks on the Neffsky Avenue and his visits to the theatre as if nothing had happened. His nose also remained in its place as if it had never quitted it. From that time he was always to be seen smiling, in a good humour, and paying attentions to pretty girls.

IV

Such was the occurrence which took place in the northern capital of our vast empire. On considering the account carefully we see that there is a good deal which looks improbable about it. Not to speak of the strange disappearance of the nose, and its appearance in different places under the disguise of a councillor of state, how was it that Kovaloff did not understand that one cannot decently advertise for a lost nose? I do not mean to say that he would have had to pay too much for the advertisement—that is a mere trifle, and I am not one of those who attach too much importance to money; but to advertise in such a case is not proper nor befitting.

Another difficulty is—how was the nose found in the baked loaf, and how did Ivan Jakovlevitch himself—no, I don't understand it at all!

But the most incomprehensible thing of all is, how authors can choose such subjects for their stories. That really surpasses my understanding. In the first place, no advantage results from it for the country; and in the second place, no harm results either.

All the same, when one reflects well, there really is something in the matter. Whatever may be said to the contrary, such cases do occur—rarely, it is true, but now and then actually.

THE AWFUL FATE OF MELPOMENUS JONES

Stephen Leacock

Some people—not you nor I, because we are so awfully self-possessed—but some people, find great difficulty in saying goodbye when making a call or spending the evening. As the moment draws near when the visitor feels that he is fairly entitled to go away he rises and says abruptly, 'Well, I think I...' Then the people say, 'Oh, must you go now? Surely it's early yet!' and a pitiful struggle ensues.

I think the saddest case of this kind of thing that I ever knew was that of my poor friend Melpomenus Jones, a curate—such a dear young man, and only twenty-three! He simply couldn't get away from people. He was too modest to tell a lie, and too religious to wish to appear rude. Now it happened that he went to call on some friends of his on the very first afternoon of his summer vacation. The next six weeks were entirely his own—absolutely nothing to do. He chatted awhile, drank two cups of tea, then braced himself for the effort and said suddenly:

'Well, I think I...'

But the lady of the house said, 'Oh, no! Mr Jones, can't you really stay a little longer?'

Jones was always truthful. 'Oh, yes,' he said, 'of course, I—er—can stay.'

'Then please don't go.'

He stayed. He drank eleven cups of tea. Night was falling. He rose again.

'Well now,' he said shyly, 'I think I really...'

'You must go?' said the lady politely. 'I thought perhaps you could have stayed to dinner...'

'Oh well, so I could, you know,' Jones said, 'if...'

'Then please stay, I'm sure my husband will be delighted.'

'All right,' he said feebly, 'I'll stay,' and he sank back into his chair, just full of tea, and miserable.

Papa came home. They had dinner. All through the meal Jones sat planning to leave at 8.30. All the family wondered whether Mr Jones was stupid and sulky, or only stupid.

After dinner mamma undertook to 'draw him out,' and showed him photographs. She showed him all the family museum, several gross of them—photos of papa's uncle and his wife, and mamma's brother and his little boy, an awfully interesting photo of papa's uncle's friend in his Bengal uniform, an awfully well-taken photo of papa's grandfather's partner's dog, and an awfully wicked one of papa as the devil for a fancy-dress ball. By 8.30 Jones had examined seventy-one photographs. There were about sixty-nine more that he hadn't. Jones rose.

'I must say good night now,' he pleaded.

'Say good night!' they said, 'why it's only half-past eight! Have you anything to do?'

'Nothing,' he admitted, and muttered something about staying six weeks, and then laughed miserably.

Just then it turned out that the favourite child of the family, such a dear little romp, had hidden Mr Jones's hat; so papa said that he must stay, and invited him to a pipe and a chat. Papa had the pipe and gave Jones the chat, and still he stayed. Every moment he meant to take the plunge, but couldn't. Then papa began to get very tired of Jones, and fidgeted and finally said, with jocular irony, that Jones had better stay all night, they could give him a shake-down. Jones mistook his meaning and thanked him with tears in his eyes, and papa put Jones to bed in the spare room and cursed him heartily.

After breakfast next day, papa went off to his work in the city, and left Jones playing with the baby, broken-hearted. His nerve was utterly gone. He was meaning to leave all day, but the thing had got on his mind and he simply couldn't. When papa came home in the evening he was surprised and chagrined to find Jones still there. He thought to jockey him out with a jest, and said he thought he'd have to charge him for his board, he! he! The unhappy young man stared wildly for a moment, then wrung papa's hand, paid him a month's board in advance, and broke down and sobbed like a child.

In the days that followed he was moody and unapproachable. He lived, of course, entirely in the drawing-room, and the lack of air and exercise began to tell sadly on his health. He passed his time in drinking tea and looking at the photographs. He would stand for hours gazing at the photographs of papa's uncle's friend in his Bengal uniform—talking to it, sometimes swearing bitterly at it. His mind was visibly failing.

At length the crash came. They carried him upstairs in a raging delirium of fever. The illness that followed was terrible. He recognized no one, not even papa's uncle's friend in his Bengal uniform. At times he would start up from his bed and shriek, 'Well, I think I...' and then fall back upon the pillow with a horrible laugh. Then, again, he would leap up and cry,

'Another cup of tea and more photographs! More photographs! Har! Har!'

At length, after a month of agony, on the last day of his vacation, he passed away. They say that when the last moment came, he sat up in bed with a beautiful smile of confidence playing upon his face, and said, 'Well—the angels are calling me; I'm afraid I really must go now. Good afternoon.'

And the rushing of his spirit from its prison-house was as rapid as a hunted cat passing over a garden fence.

THE HAUNTED HOUSE

Charles Dickens

Under none of the accredited ghostly circumstances, and environed by none of the conventional ghostly surroundings, did I first make acquaintance with the house which is the subject of this Christmas piece. I saw it in the daylight, with the sun upon it. There was no wind, no rain, no lightning, no thunder, no awful or unwonted circumstance, of any kind, to heighten its effect. More than that, I had come to it direct from a railway station: it was not more than a mile distant from the railway station; and, as I stood outside the house, looking back upon the way I had come, I could see the goods train running smoothly along the embankment in the valley. I will not say that everything was utterly commonplace, because I doubt if anything can be that, except to utterly commonplace people—and there my vanity steps in; but, I will take it on myself to say that anybody might see the house as I saw it, any fine autumn morning.

The manner of my lighting on it was this.

I was travelling towards London out of the North, intending to stop by the way, to look at the house. My health required a temporary residence in the country; and a friend of mine who knew that, and who had happened to drive past the house, had written to me to suggest it as a likely place. I had got into the train at midnight, and had fallen asleep, and had woke up and had sat looking out of window at the brilliant Northern Lights in the sky, and had fallen asleep again, and had woke up again to find the night gone, with the usual discontented conviction on me that I hadn't been to sleep at all—upon which question, in the first imbecility of that condition, I am ashamed to believe that I would have done wager by battle with the man who sat opposite me. That opposite man had had, through the night—as that opposite man always has—several legs too many, and all of them too long. In addition to this unreasonable conduct (which was only to be expected of him), he had had a pencil and a pocket-book, and had been perpetually listening and taking notes. It had appeared to me that these aggravating notes related to the jolts and bumps of the carriage, and I should have resigned myself to his taking them, under a general supposition that he was in the civil-engineering way of life, if he had not sat staring straight over my head whenever he listened. He was a goggle-eyed gentleman of a perplexed aspect, and his demeanour became unbearable.

It was a cold, dead morning (the sun not being up yet), and when I had out-watched the paling light of the fires of the iron country, and the curtain of heavy smoke that hung at once between me and the stars and between me and the day, I turned to my fellow-traveller and said:

'I beg your pardon, sir, but do you observe anything particular in me?' For, really, he appeared to be taking down, either my travelling-cap or my hair, with a minuteness that was a liberty.

The goggle-eyed gentleman withdrew his eyes from behind

me, as if the back of the carriage were a hundred miles off, and said, with a lofty look of compassion for my insignificance:

'In you, sir?—B.'

'B, sir?' said I, growing warm.

'I have nothing to do with you, sir,' returned the gentleman; 'pray let me listen—O.'

He enunciated this vowel after a pause, and noted it down.

At first I was alarmed, for an Express lunatic and no communication with the guard, is a serious position. The thought came to my relief that the gentleman might be what is popularly called a 'Rapper': one of a sect for (some of) whom I have the highest respect, but whom I don't believe in. I was going to ask him the question, when he took the bread out of my mouth.

'You will excuse me,' said the gentleman contemptuously, 'if I am too much in advance of common humanity to trouble myself at all about it. I have passed the night—as indeed I pass the whole of my time now—in spiritual intercourse.'

'O!' said I, somewhat snappishly.

'The conferences of the night began,' continued the gentleman, turning several leaves of his note-book, 'with this message: "Evil communications corrupt good manners."'

'Sound,' said I; 'but, absolutely new?'

'New from spirits,' returned the gentleman.

I could only repeat my rather snappish 'O!' and ask if I might be favoured with the last communication.

'A bird in the hand,' said the gentleman, reading his last entry with great solemnity, 'is worth two in the Bosh.'

'Truly I am of the same opinion,' said I; 'but shouldn't it be Bush?'

'It came to me, Bosh,' returned the gentleman.

The gentleman then informed me that the spirit of Socrates had delivered this special revelation in the course of the night. 'My friend, I hope you are pretty well. There are two in this railway carriage. How do you do? There are seventeen thousand four hundred and seventy-nine spirits here, but you cannot see them. Pythagoras is here. He is not at liberty to mention it, but hopes you like travelling.' Galileo likewise had dropped in, with this scientific intelligence. 'I am glad to see you, amico. Come stai? Water will freeze when it is cold enough. Addio!' In the course of the night, also, the following phenomena had occurred. Bishop Butler had insisted on spelling his name, 'Bubler,' for which offence against orthography and good manners he had been dismissed as out of temper. John Milton (suspected of wilful mystification) had repudiated the authorship of *Paradise Lost*, and had introduced, as joint authors of that poem, two unknown gentlemen, respectively named Grungers and Scadgingtone. And Prince Arthur, nephew of King John of England, had described himself as tolerably comfortable in the seventh circle, where he was learning to paint on velvet, under the direction of Mrs Trimmer and Mary Queen of Scots.

If this should meet the eye of the gentleman who favoured me with these disclosures, I trust he will excuse my confessing that the sight of the rising sun, and the contemplation of the magnificent order of the vast Universe, made me impatient of them. In a word, I was so impatient of them, that I was mightily glad to get out at the next station, and to exchange these clouds and vapours for the free air of Heaven.

By that time it was a beautiful morning. As I walked away among such leaves as had already fallen from the golden, brown, and russet trees; and as I looked around me on the wonders of Creation, and thought of the steady, unchanging, and harmonious laws by which they are sustained; the gentleman's spiritual intercourse seemed to me as poor a piece of journey-work as ever this world saw. In which heathen state of mind, I came within view of the house, and stopped to examine it attentively.

It was a solitary house, standing in a sadly neglected garden: a pretty even square of some two acres. It was a house of about the time of George the Second; as stiff, as cold, as formal, and in as bad taste, as could possibly be desired by the most loyal admirer of the whole quartet of Georges. It was uninhabited, but had, within a year or two, been cheaply repaired to render it habitable; I say cheaply, because the work had been done in a surface manner, and was already decaying as to the paint and plaster, though the colours were fresh. A lopsided board drooped over the garden wall, announcing that it was 'to let on very reasonable terms, well furnished.' It was much too closely and heavily shadowed by trees, and, in particular, there were six tall poplars before the front windows, which were excessively melancholy, and the site of which had been extremely ill chosen.

It was easy to see that it was an avoided house—a house that was shunned by the village, to which my eye was guided by a church spire some half a mile off—a house that nobody would take. And the natural inference was, that it had the reputation of being a haunted house.

No period within the four-and-twenty hours of day and night is so solemn to me, as the early morning. In the summer-time, I often rise very early, and repair to my room to do a day's work before breakfast, and I am always on those occasions deeply impressed by the stillness and solitude around me. Besides that there is something awful in the being surrounded by familiar faces asleep—in the knowledge that those who are dearest to us and to whom we are dearest, are profoundly unconscious of us, in an impassive state, anticipative of that mysterious condition to which we are all tending—the stopped life, the broken threads of yesterday, the deserted seat, the closed book, the unfinished but abandoned occupation, all are images of Death. The tranquillity of the hour is the tranquillity of Death. The colour and the chill have the same association. Even a certain air that familiar household objects take upon them when they first emerge from the shadows of the night into the morning, of being newer, and as they used to be long ago, has its counterpart in the subsidence of the worn face of maturity or age, in death, into the old youthful look. Moreover, I once saw the apparition of my father, at this hour. He was alive and well, and nothing ever came of it, but I saw him in the daylight, sitting with his back towards me, on a seat that stood beside my bed. His head was resting on his hand, and whether he was slumbering or grieving, I could not discern. Amazed to see him there, I sat up, moved my position, leaned out of bed, and watched him. As he did not move, I spoke to him more than once. As he did not move then, I became alarmed and laid my hand upon his shoulder, as I thought—and there was no such thing.

For all these reasons, and for others less easily and briefly statable, I find the early morning to be my most ghostly time. Any house would be more or less haunted, to me, in the early morning; and a haunted house could scarcely address me to greater advantage than then.

I walked on into the village, with the desertion of this house upon my mind, and I found the landlord of the little inn, sanding his doorstep. I bespoke breakfast, and broached the subject of the house.

'Is it haunted?' I asked.

The landlord looked at me, shook his head, and answered, 'I say nothing.'

'Then it is haunted?'

'Well!' cried the landlord, in an outburst of frankness that had the appearance of desperation—'I wouldn't sleep in it.'

'Why not?'

'If I wanted to have all the bells in a house ring, with nobody to ring 'em; and all the doors in a house bang, with nobody to bang 'em; and all sorts of feet treading about, with no feet there; why, then,' said the landlord, 'I'd sleep in that house.'

'Is anything seen there?'

The landlord looked at me again, and then, with his former appearance of desperation, called down his stable-yard for 'Ikey!'

The call produced a high-shouldered young fellow, with a round red face, a short crop of sandy hair, a very broad humorous mouth, a turned-up nose, and a great sleeved waistcoat of purple bars, with mother-of-pearl buttons, that seemed to be growing upon him, and to be in a fair way—if it were not pruned—of covering his head and overrunning his boots.

'This gentleman wants to know,' said the landlord, 'if anything's seen at the Poplars.'

'Ooded woman with a howl,' said Ikey, in a state of great freshness.

'Do you mean a cry?'

'I mean a bird, sir.'

'A hooded woman with an owl. Dear me! Did you ever see her?'

'I seen the howl.'

'Never the woman?'

'Not so plain as the howl, but they always keeps together.'

'Has anybody ever seen the woman as plainly as the owl?'

'Lord bless you, sir! Lots.'

'Who?'

'Lord bless you, sir! Lots.'

'The general-dealer opposite, for instance, who is opening his shop?'

'Perkins? Bless you, Perkins wouldn't go a-nigh the place. No!' observed the young man, with considerable feeling; 'He ain't overwise, ain't Perkins, but he ain't such a fool as that.'

(Here, the landlord murmured his confidence in Perkins's knowing better.)

'Who is—or who was—the hooded woman with the owl? Do you know?'

'Well!' said Ikey, holding up his cap with one hand while he scratched his head with the other, 'they say, in general, that she was murdered, and the howl he "ooted the while".'

This very concise summary of the facts was all I could learn, except that a young man, as hearty and likely a young man as ever I see, had been took with fits and held down in 'em, after seeing the hooded woman. Also, that a personage, dimly described as 'a hold chap, a sort of one-eyed tramp, answering to the name of Joby, unless you challenged him as Greenwood, and then he said, "Why not? And even if so, mind your own business,"' had encountered the hooded woman, a matter of five or six times. But, I was not materially assisted by these witnesses: inasmuch as the first was in California, and the last was, as Ikey said (and he was confirmed by the landlord), 'anywhere'.

Now, although I regard with a hushed and solemn fear, the mysteries, between which and this state of existence is interposed the barrier of the great trial and change that fall on all the things that live; and although I have not the audacity to pretend that I know anything of them; I can no more reconcile the mere banging of doors, ringing of bells, creaking of boards, and such-like insignificances, with the majestic beauty and pervading analogy of all the divine rules that I am permitted to understand, than I had been able, a little while before, to yoke the spiritual intercourse of my fellow traveller to the chariot of the rising sun. Moreover, I had lived in two haunted houses— both abroad. In one of these, an old Italian palace, which bore the reputation of being very badly haunted indeed, and which had recently been twice abandoned on that account, I lived eight months, most tranquilly and pleasantly: notwithstanding that the house had a score of mysterious bedrooms, which were never used, and possessed, in one large room in which I sat reading, times out of number at all hours, and next to which I slept, a haunted chamber of the first pretensions. I gently hinted these considerations to the landlord. And as to this particular house having a bad name, I reasoned with him, 'Why, how many things had bad names undeservedly, and how easy it was to give bad names, and did he not think that if he and I were persistently to whisper in the village that any weird-looking old drunken tinker of the neighbourhood had sold himself to the Devil, he would come in time to be suspected of that commercial venture!' All this wise talk was perfectly ineffective with the landlord, I am bound to confess, and was as dead a failure as ever I made in my life.

To cut this part of the story short, I was piqued about the haunted house, and was already half resolved to take it. So, after breakfast, I got the keys from Perkins's brother-in-law (a whip and harness-maker, who keeps the Post Office, and is under submission to a most rigorous wife of the Doubly Seceding Little Emmanuel persuasion), and went up to the house, attended by my landlord and by Ikey.

Within, I found it, as I had expected, transcendently dismal. The slowly changing shadows waved on it from the heavy trees, were doleful in the last degree; the house was ill-placed, ill-built, ill-planned and ill-fitted. It was damp, it was not free from dry rot, there was a flavour of rats in it, and it was the gloomy victim of that indescribable decay which settles on all the work of man's hands whenever it's not turned to man's account. The kitchens and offices were too large, and too remote from each other. Above stairs and below, waste tracts of passage intervened between patches of fertility represented by rooms; and there was a mouldy old well with a green growth upon it, hiding like a murderous trap, near the bottom of the back-stairs, under the double row of bells. One of these bells was labelled, on a black ground in faded white letters, 'Master B.' This, they told me, was the bell that rang the most.

'Who was Master B.?' I asked. 'Is it known what he did while the owl hooted?'

'Rang the bell,' said Ikey.

I was rather struck by the prompt dexterity with which this young man pitched his fur cap at the bell, and rang it himself. It was a loud, unpleasant bell, and made a very disagreeable sound. The other bells were inscribed according to the names of the rooms to which their wires were conducted: as 'Picture Room,' 'Double Room,' 'Clock Room,' and the like. Following Master B.'s bell to its source I found that young gentleman to have had but indifferent third-class accommodation in a triangular cabin under the cock-loft, with a corner fireplace which Master B. must have been exceedingly small if he were ever able to warm himself at, and a corner chimney piece like a pyramidal staircase to the ceiling for Tom Thumb. The papering of one side of the room had dropped down bodily, with fragments of plaster adhering to it, and almost blocked up the door. It appeared that Master B., in his spiritual condition, always made a point of pulling the paper down. Neither the landlord nor Ikey could suggest why he made such a fool of himself.

Except that the house had an immensely large rambling loft at top, I made no other discoveries. It was moderately well furnished, but sparely. Some of the furniture—say, a third—was as old as the house; the rest was of various periods within the last half-century. I was referred to a corn-chandler in the market-place of the county town to treat for the house. I went that day, and I took it for six months.

It was just the middle of October when I moved in with my maiden sister (I venture to call her eight-and-thirty, she is so very handsome, sensible and engaging). We took with us, a deaf stable-man, my bloodhound Turk, two women servants, and a young person called an Odd Girl. I have reason to record of the attendant last enumerated, who was one of the Saint Lawrence's Union Female Orphans, that she was a fatal mistake and a disastrous engagement.

The year was dying early, the leaves were falling fast, it was a raw cold day when we took possession, and the gloom of the house was most depressing. The cook (an amiable woman, but of a weak turn of intellect) burst into tears on beholding the kitchen, and requested that her silver watch might be delivered over to her sister (2 Tuppintock's Gardens, Liggs's Walk, Clapham Rise), in the event of anything happening to her from the damp. Streaker, the housemaid, feigned cheerfulness, but was the greater martyr. The Odd Girl, who had never been in the country, alone was pleased, and made arrangements for sowing an acorn in the garden outside the scullery window, and rearing an oak.

We went, before dark, through all the natural—as opposed to supernatural—miseries incidental to our state. Dispiriting reports ascended (like the smoke) from the basement in volumes, and descended from the upper rooms. There was no rolling-pin, there was no salamander (which failed to surprise me, for I don't know what it is), there was nothing in the house, what there was, was broken, the last people must have lived like pigs, what could the meaning of the landlord be? Through these distresses, the Odd Girl was cheerful and exemplary. But within four hours after dark we had got into a supernatural groove, and the Odd Girl had seen 'Eyes', and was in hysterics.

My sister and I had agreed to keep the haunting strictly to ourselves, and my impression was, and still is, that I had not left Ikey, when he helped to unload the cart, alone with the women, or any one of them, for one minute. Nevertheless, as I say, the Odd Girl had 'seen Eyes' (no other explanation could ever be drawn from her), before nine, and by ten o'clock had had as much vinegar applied to her as would pickle a handsome salmon.

I leave a discerning public to judge of my feelings, when, under these untoward circumstances, at about half-past ten o'clock Master B.'s bell began to ring in a most infuriated manner, and Turk howled until the house resounded with his lamentations!

I hope I may never again be in a state of mind so unchristian as the mental frame in which I lived for some weeks, respecting the memory of Master B. Whether his bell was rung by rats, or mice, or bats, or wind, or what other accidental vibration, or sometimes by one cause, sometimes another, and sometimes by collusion, I don't know; but, certain it is, that it did ring two nights out of three, until I conceived the happy idea of twisting Master B.'s neck—in other words, breaking his bell short off—and silencing that young gentleman, as to my experience and belief, forever.

But, by that time, the Odd Girl had developed such improving powers of catalepsy, that she had become a shining example of that very inconvenient disorder. She would stiffen, like a Guy Fawkes endowed with unreason, on the most irrelevant occasions. I would address the servants in a lucid manner, pointing out to them that I had painted Master B.'s room and balked the paper, and taken Master B.'s bell away and balked the ringing, and if they could suppose that that confounded boy had lived and died, to clothe himself with no better behaviour than would most unquestionably have brought him and the sharpest particles of a birch-broom into close acquaintance in the present imperfect state of existence, could they also suppose a mere poor human being, such as I was, capable by those contemptible means of counteracting and limiting the powers of the disembodied spirits of the dead, or of any spirits?—I say I would become emphatic and cogent, not to say rather complacent, in such an address, when it would all go for nothing by reason of the Odd Girl's suddenly stiffening from the toes upward, and glaring among us like a parochial petrifaction.

Streaker, the housemaid, too, had an attribute of a most discomfiting nature. I am unable to say whether she was of an usually lymphatic temperament, or what else was the matter with her, but this young woman became a mere distillery for the production of the largest and most transparent tears I ever met with. Combined with these characteristics, was a peculiar tenacity of hold in those specimens, so that they didn't fall, but hung upon her face and nose. In this condition, and mildly and deplorably shaking her head, her silence would throw me more heavily than the Admirable Crichton could have done in a verbal disputation for a purse of money. Cook, likewise, always covered me with confusion as with a garment, by neatly winding up the session with the protest that the Ouse was wearing her out, and by meekly repeating her last wishes regarding her silver watch.

As to our nightly life, the contagion of suspicion and fear was among us, and there is no such contagion under the sky. Hooded woman? According to the accounts, we were in a perfect Convent of hooded women. Noises? With that contagion downstairs, I myself have sat in the dismal parlour, listening, until I have heard so many and such strange noises, that they would have chilled my blood if I had not warmed it by dashing out to make discoveries. Try this in bed, in the dead of the night: try this at your own comfortable fire-side, in the life of the night. You can fill any house with noises, if you will, until you have a noise for every nerve in your nervous system.

I repeat; the contagion of suspicion and fear was among us, and there is no such contagion under the sky. The women (their noses in a chronic state of excoriation from smelling-salts) were always primed and loaded for a swoon, and ready to go off with hair-triggers. The two elder detached the Odd Girl on all expeditions that were considered doubly hazardous, and she always established the reputation of such adventures by coming back cataleptic. If Cook or Streaker went overhead after dark, we knew we should presently hear a bump on the ceiling; and this took place so constantly, that it was as if a fighting man were engaged to go about the house, administering a touch of his art which I believe is called 'The Auctioneer', to every domestic he met with.

It was in vain to do anything. It was in vain to be frightened, for the moment in one's own person, by a real owl, and then to show the owl. It was in vain to discover, by striking an accidental discord on the piano, that Turk always howled at particular notes and combinations. It was in vain to be a Rhadamanthus with the bells, and if an unfortunate bell rang without leave, to have it down inexorably and silence it. It was in vain to fire up chimneys, let torches down the well, charge furiously into suspected rooms and recesses. We changed servants, and it was no better. The new set ran away, and a third set came, and it was no better. At last, our comfortable housekeeping got to be so disorganized and wretched, that I one night dejectedly said to my sister: 'Patty, I begin to despair of our getting people to go on with us here, and I think we must give this up.'

My sister, who is a woman of immense spirit, replied, 'No, John, don't give it up. Don't be beaten, John. There is another way.'

'And what is that?' said I.

'John,' returned my sister, 'if we are not to be driven out of this house, and that for no reason whatever, that is apparent to you or me, we must help ourselves and take the house wholly and solely into our own hands.'

'But, the servants,' said I.

'Have no servants,' said my sister, boldly.

Like most people in my grade of life, I had never thought of the possibility of going on without those faithful obstructions. The notion was so new to me when suggested, that I looked very doubtful. 'We know they come here to be frightened and infect one another, and we know they are frightened and do infect one another,' said my sister.

'With the exception of Bottles,' I observed, in a meditative tone.

(The deaf stable-man. I kept him in my service, and still keep him, as a phenomenon of moroseness not to be matched in England.)

'To be sure, John,' assented my sister, 'except Bottles. And what does that go to prove? Bottles talks to nobody, and hears nobody unless he is absolutely roared at, and what alarm has Bottles ever given, or taken! None.'

This was perfectly true; the individual in question having retired, every night at ten o'clock, to his bed over the coach-house, with no other company than a pitchfork and a pail of water. That the pail of water would have been over me, and the pitchfork through me, if I had put myself without announcement in Bottles's way after that minute, I had deposited in my own mind as a fact worth remembering. Neither had Bottles ever taken the least notice of any of our many uproars. An imperturbable and speechless man, he had sat at his supper, with Streaker present in a swoon, and the Odd Girl marble, and had only put another potato in his cheek, or profited by the general misery to help himself to beefsteak pie.

'And so,' continued my sister, 'I exempt Bottles. And considering, John, that the house is too large, and perhaps too lonely, to be kept well in hand by Bottles, you, and me, I propose that we cast about among our friends for a certain selected number of the most reliable and willing—form a society here for three months—wait upon ourselves and one another—live cheerfully and socially—and see what happens.'

I was so charmed with my sister, that I embraced her on the spot, and went into her plan with the greatest ardour.

We were then in the third week of November; but, we took our measures so vigorously, and were so well seconded by the friends in whom we confided, that there was still a week of the month unexpired, when our party all came down together merrily, and mustered in the haunted house.

I will mention, in this place, two small changes that I made while my sister and I were yet alone. It occurring to me as not improbable that Turk howled in the house at night, partly because he wanted to get out of it, I stationed him in his kennel outside, but unchained; and I seriously warned the village that any man who came in his way must not expect to leave him without a rip in his own throat. I then casually asked Ikey if he were a judge of a gun? On his saying, 'Yes, sir, I knows a good gun when I sees her,' I begged the favour of his stepping up to the house and looking at mine.

'She's a true one, sir,' said Ikey, after inspecting a double-barrelled rifle that I bought in New York a few years ago. 'No mistake about her, sir.'

'Ikey,' said I, 'don't mention it; I have seen something in this house.'

'No, sir?' he whispered, greedily opening his eyes. 'Ooded lady, sir?'

'Don't be frightened,' said I. 'It was a figure rather like you.'

'Lord, sir?'

'Ikey!' said I, shaking hands with him warmly: I may say affectionately, 'If there is any truth in these ghost-stories, the greatest service I can do you, is, to fire at that figure. And I promise you, by Heaven and earth, I will do it with this gun if I see it again!'

The young man thanked me, and took his leave with some little precipitation, after declining a glass of liquor. I imparted my secret to him, because I had never quite forgotten his throwing his cap at the bell; because I had, on another occasion, noticed something very like a fur cap, lying not far from the bell, one night when it had burst out ringing; and because I had remarked that we were at our ghostliest whenever he came up in the evening to comfort the servants. Let me do Ikey no injustice. He was afraid of the house, and believed in its being haunted; and yet he would play false on the haunting side, so surely as he got an opportunity. The Odd Girl's case was exactly similar. She went about the house in a state of real terror, and yet lied monstrously and wilfully, and invented many of the alarms she spread, and made many of the sounds we heard. I had had my eye on the two, and I know it. It is not necessary for me, here, to account for this preposterous state of mind; I content myself with remarking that it is familiarly known to every intelligent man who has had fair medical, legal, or other watchful experience; that it is as well established and as common a state of mind as any with which observers are acquainted; and that it is one of the first elements, above all others, rationally to be suspected in, and strictly looked for, and separated from, any question of this kind.

To return to our party. The first thing we did when we were all assembled, was, to draw lots for bedrooms. That done, and every bedroom, and, indeed, the whole house, having been minutely examined by the whole body, we allotted the various household duties, as if we had been on a gipsy party, or a yachting party, or a hunting party, or were shipwrecked. I then recounted the floating rumours concerning the hooded lady, the owl, and Master B.: with others, still more filmy, which had floated about during our occupation, relative to some ridiculous old ghost of the female gender who went up and down, carrying the ghost of a round table; and also to an impalpable jackass, whom nobody was ever able to catch. Some of these ideas I really believe our people below had communicated to one another in some diseased way, without conveying them in words. We then gravely called one another to witness, that we were not there to be deceived, or to deceive—which we considered pretty much the same thing—and that, with a serious sense of responsibility, we would be strictly true to one another, and would strictly follow out the truth. The understanding was established, that any one who heard unusual noises in the night, and who wished to trace them, should knock at my door; lastly, that on Twelfth Night, the last night of holy Christmas, all our individual experiences since that then present hour of our coming together in the haunted house, should be brought to light for the good of all; and that we would hold our peace on the subject till then, unless on some remarkable provocation to break silence.

We were, in number and in character, as follows:

First—to get my sister and myself out of the way—there were we two. In the drawing of lots, my sister drew her own room, and I drew Master B.'s. Next, there was our first cousin John Herschel, so called after the great astronomer: than whom I suppose a better man at a telescope does not breathe. With him, was his wife: a charming creature to whom he had been married in the previous spring. I thought it (under the circumstances) rather imprudent to bring her, because there is no knowing what even a false alarm may do at such a time; but I suppose he knew his own business best, and I must say that if she had been my wife, I never could have left her endearing and bright face behind. They drew the Clock Room. Alfred Starling, an uncommonly agreeable young fellow of eight-and-twenty for whom I have the greatest liking, was in the Double Room; mine, usually, and designated by that name from having a dressing-room within it, with two large and cumbersome windows, which no wedges I was ever able to make, would keep from shaking, in any weather, wind or no wind. Alfred is a young fellow who pretends to be 'fast' (another word for loose, as I understand the term), but who is much too good and sensible for that nonsense, and who would have distinguished himself before now, if his father had not unfortunately left him a small independence of two hundred a year, on the strength of which his only occupation in life has been to spend six. I am in hopes, however, that his banker may break, or that he may enter into some speculation guaranteed to pay twenty per cent; for, I am convinced that if he could only be ruined, his fortune is made. Belinda Bates, bosom friend of my sister, and a most intellectual, amiable, and delightful girl, got the Picture Room. She has a fine genius for poetry, combined with real business earnestness, and 'goes in'—to use an expression of Alfred's—for Woman's mission, Woman's rights, Woman's wrongs, and everything that is woman's with a capital W, or is not and ought to be, or is and ought not to be. 'Most praiseworthy, my dear, and Heaven prosper you!' I whispered to her on the first night of my taking leave of her at the Picture-Room door, 'but don't overdo it. And in respect of the great necessity there is, my darling, for more employments being within the reach of Woman than our civilization has as yet assigned to her, don't fly at the unfortunate men, even those men who are at first sight in your way, as if they were the natural oppressors of your sex; for, trust me, Belinda, they do sometimes spend their wages among wives and daughters, sisters, mothers, aunts and grandmothers; and the play is, really, not all Wolf and Red Riding-Hood, but has other parts in it.' However, I digress.

Belinda, as I have mentioned, occupied the Picture Room. We had but three other chambers: the Corner Room, the

Cupboard Room, and the Garden Room. My old friend, Jack
Governor, 'slung his hammock,' as he called it, in the Corner
Room. I have always regarded Jack as the finest-looking sailor
that ever sailed. He is gray now, but as handsome as he was
a quarter of a century ago—nay, handsomer. A portly, cheery,
well-built figure of a broad-shouldered man, with a frank smile,
a brilliant dark eye, and a rich dark eyebrow. I remember those
under darker hair, and they look all the better for their silver
setting. He has been wherever his Union namesake flies, has Jack,
and I have met old shipmates of his, away in the Mediterranean
and on the other side of the Atlantic, who have beamed and
brightened at the casual mention of his name, and have cried,
'You know Jack Governor? Then you know a prince of men!'
That he is! And so unmistakably a naval officer, that if you
were to meet him coming out of an Esquimaux snow-hut in
seal's skin, you would be vaguely persuaded he was in full
naval uniform.

Jack once had that bright clear eye of his on my sister;
but, it fell out that he married another lady and took her to
South America, where she died. This was a dozen years ago or
more. He brought down with him to our haunted house a little
cask of salt beef; for, he is always convinced that all salt beef
not of his own pickling, is mere carrion, and invariably, when
he goes to London, packs a piece in his portmanteau. He had
also volunteered to bring with him one 'Nat Beaver,' an old
comrade of his, captain of a merchantman. Mr Beaver, with a
thick-set wooden face and figure, and apparently as hard as a
block all over, proved to be an intelligent man, with a world of
watery experiences in him, and great practical knowledge. At
times, there was a curious nervousness about him, apparently
the lingering result of some old illness; but, it seldom lasted

many minutes. He got the Cupboard Room, and lay there next to Mr Undery, my friend and solicitor: who came down, in an amateur capacity, 'to go through with it,' as he said, and who plays whist better than the whole Law List, from the red cover at the beginning to the red cover at the end.

I never was happier in my life, and I believe it was the universal feeling among us. Jack Governor, always a man of wonderful resources, was chief cook, and made some of the best dishes I ever ate, including unapproachable curries. My sister was pastrycook and confectioner. Starling and I were cook's mate, turn and turn about, and on special occasions the chief cook 'pressed' Mr Beaver. We had a great deal of outdoor sport and exercise, but nothing was neglected within, and there was no ill-humour or misunderstanding among us, and our evenings were so delightful that we had at least one good reason for being reluctant to go to bed.

We had a few night alarms in the beginning. On the first night, I was knocked up by Jack with a most wonderful ship's lantern in his hand, like the gills of some monster of the deep, who informed me that he 'was going aloft to the main truck,' to have the weathercock down. It was a stormy night and I remonstrated; but Jack called my attention to its making a sound like a cry of despair, and said somebody would be 'hailing a ghost' presently, if it wasn't done. So, up to the top of the house, where I could hardly stand for the wind, we went, accompanied by Mr Beaver; and there Jack, lantern and all, with Mr Beaver after him, swarmed up to the top of a cupola, some two dozen feet above the chimneys, and stood upon nothing particular, coolly knocking the weathercock off, until they both got into such good spirits with the wind and the height, that I thought they would never come down. Another night, they turned out again, and had a chimney-cowl off. Another night, they cut a sobbing and gulping water pipe away. Another night, they found out something else. On several occasions, they both, in the coolest manner, simultaneously dropped out of their respective bedroom windows, hand over hand by their counterpanes, to 'overhaul' something mysterious in the garden.

The engagement among us was faithfully kept, and nobody revealed anything. All we knew was, if any one's room were haunted, no one looked the worse for it.

The Zigzag Walk

Ruskin Bond

Uncle Ken always maintained that the best way to succeed in life was to zigzag. 'If you keep going off in new directions,' he declared, 'you will meet new career opportunities!'

Well, opportunities certainly came Uncle Ken's way, but he was not a success in the sense that Dale Carnegie or Deepak Chopra would have defined a successful man...

In a long life devoted to 'muddling through' with the help of the family, Uncle Ken's many projects had included a chicken farm (rather like the one operated by Ukridge in Wodehouse's *Love Among the Chickens*) and a mineral water bottling project. For this latter enterprise, he bought a thousand soda-water bottles and filled them with sulphur water from the springs five miles from Dehra. It was good stuff, taken in small quantities, but drunk one bottle at a time it proved corrosive—'sulphur and brimstone' as one irate customer described it—and angry buyers demonstrated in front of the house, throwing empty bottles over the wall into Grandmother's garden.

Grandmother was furious—more with Uncle Ken than with the demonstrators—and made him give everyone's money back.

'You have to be healthy and strong to take sulphur water,'

he explained later.

'I thought it was supposed to snake you healthy and strong,' I said.

Grandfather remarked that it did not compare with plain soda-water, which he took with his whisky. 'Why don't you just bottle soda-water?' he said. 'There's a much bigger demand for it.'

But Uncle Ken believed that he had to be original in all things.

'The secret to success is to zigzag,' he said. 'You certainly zigzagged round the garden when your customers were throwing their bottles back at you,' said Grandmother.

Uncle Ken also invented the zigzag walk.

The only way you could really come to know a place well, was to walk in a truly haphazard way. To make a zigzag walk you take the first turning to the left, the first to the right, then the first to the left and so on. It can be quite fascinating provided you are in no hurry to reach your destination. The trouble was that Uncle Ken used this zigzag method even when he had a train to catch.

When Grandmother asked him to go to the station to meet Aunt Mabel who was arriving from Lucknow, he zigzagged through town, taking in the botanical gardens in the west and the limestone factories to the east, finally reaching the station by way of the goods yard, in order, as he said, 'to take it by surprise'.

Nobody was surprised, least of all Aunt Mabel who had taken a tonga and reached the house while Uncle Ken was still sitting on the station platform, waiting for the next train to come in. I was sent to fetch him.

'Let's zigzag home again,' he said.

'Only on one condition, we eat chaat every fifteen minutes,' I said.

So we went home by way of all the most winding bazaars, and in North Indian towns they do tend to zigzag, stopping at numerous chaat and halwai shops, until Uncle Ken had finished his money. We got home very late and were scolded by everyone; but as Uncle Ken told me, we were pioneers and had to expect to be misunderstood and even maligned. Posterity would recognize the true value of zigzagging.

'The zigzag way,' he said, 'is the diagonal between heart and reason.'

In our more troubled times, had he taken to preaching on the subject, he might have acquired a large following of dropouts. But Uncle Ken was the original dropout. He would not have tolerated others.

Had he been a space traveller he would have gone from star to star, zigzagging across the Milky Way.

Uncle Ken would not have succeeded in getting anywhere very fast, but I think he did succeed in getting at least one convert (myself) to see his point: 'When you zigzag, you are not choosing what to see in this world but you are giving the world a chance to see you!'